AIRPORT CODE RED

JAMES PATTERSON is one of the best-known and biggest-selling writers of all time. His books have sold in excess of 300 million copies worldwide and he has been the most borrowed author in UK libraries for the past nine years in a row. He is the author of some of the most popular series of the past two decades – the Alex Cross, Women's Murder Club, Detective Michael Bennett and Private novels – and he has written many other number one bestsellers including romance novels and stand-alone thrillers.

James is passionate about encouraging children to read. Inspired by his own son who was a reluctant reader, he also writes a range of books for young readers including the Middle School, I Funny, Treasure Hunters, House of Robots, Confessions and Maximum Ride series. James is the proud sponsor of the World Book Day Award and has donated millions in grants
He lives in Florida with his

BOOK**SHOTS**

STORIES AT THE SPEED OF LIFE

What you are holding in your hands right now is no ordinary book, it's a BookShot.

BookShots are page-turning stories by James Patterson and other writers that can be read in one sitting.

Each and every one is fast-paced, 100% story-driven; a shot of pure entertainment guaranteed to satisfy.

Available as new, compact paperbacks, ebooks and audio, everywhere books are sold.

BookShots – the ultimate form of storytelling. From the ultimate storyteller.

AIRPORT
CODE RED

JAMES PATTERSON

WITH MICHAEL WHITE

BOOKSHOTS

1 3 5 7 9 10 8 6 4 2

BookShots
20 Vauxhall Bridge Road
London SW1V 2SA

BookShots is part of the Penguin Random House
group of companies whose addresses can be found at
global.penguinrandomhouse.com

First published by BookShots in 2016

www.penguin.co.uk

A CIP catalogue record for this book is available
from the British Library.

ISBN 9781786530370

Typeset in Garamond Premier Pro font 11/15.5 pt in
India by Thomson Digital Pvt Ltd, Noida Delhi

Printed and bound in Great Britain by Clays Ltd, St Ives Plc

AIRPORT
CODE RED

CHAPTER 1

Bradford, England, Tuesday evening

'*Allahu Akbar! Allahu Akbar!*' shouted Ilham Al-Yussuv. He was dressed in combat fatigues and strutted in front of a group of forty-one men. They screamed back: '*ALLAHU AKBAR! ALLAHU AKBAR!*'

Al-Yussuv turned to his right. His wife, Hubab Essa, a woman almost as tall as him, who was wearing a black robe and black headscarf, nodded, her expression blank. Kneeling at her feet was a young man. He was blindfolded; sweat ran down his cheeks and into the open collar of his shirt. The couple pulled on masks and Al-Yussuv nodded to a man videoing them.

'This is James Dalton,' Al-Yussuv said to the camera, pointing to the shaking prisoner. 'A student from Nottingham University. He has been found guilty of mocking the Holy Book and shall be punished.' He nodded to his wife. Hubab Essa stepped forward, pulling a Walther PPK from a pocket in her robe. She placed it against the back of Dalton's head and pulled the trigger. The prisoner fell forward and the crowd of men cheered and shouted in jubilation. A few were waving guns and knives over their heads. The man with the video camera kept recording the two masked leaders.

Essa stepped beside James Dalton's dead body and spat on it. Then she raised her head, wiped her mouth and put up her hands. 'Silence. Silence, my brothers. This is but the start,' she said with quiet menace, then looked round at the gathering. 'I am not a woman. I am a *Muslim*. I am a jihadist. A holy warrior. I am the Infidel's worst nightmare.'

CHAPTER 2

THE TERRORIST CELL HAD been in Numbers 54 and 56 Glimmer Street, Bradford, for ten days. Combined, the two derelict properties served as a perfect safe house. They were the last buildings still standing on a street two miles from the centre of Bradford, and were set for demolition in two weeks. The houses were off the grid, listed in some city council office computer file but ignored by everyone. Everyone, that is, except the forty-two men and one woman who had suffered squalid conditions for ten days and were waiting to spring into action. There was no running water, electricity came from a small generator in the backyard of each house and there were more rats than there were humans. Apart from the cell's leaders, Al-Yussuv and Essa, the jihadists had no sanitation or privacy whatsoever. If any members of the cell needed to leave the street, they wore disguises and travelled by public transport. They never hung out in groups and they always left and returned via different routes.

Morale was ebbing. That was part of the reason for Tuesday evening's entertainment with the captured Nottingham University student, the eighteen-year-old son of a baker, originally from

London, who had been visiting friends in Bradford. During his short lifetime, James Dalton had barely seen a copy of the Quran, let alone insulted it.

Al-Yussuv and Essa had a small room to themselves at the rear of Number 54. Their men were spread out over a dozen other rooms in the two decrepit houses. It was late, quiet.

'The show was a success, husband,' Essa said as they sat on the edge of the mattress on the floor. 'It served a double purpose. Saabiq has uploaded the film already and it's been passed through half a dozen servers and IP addresses. It's completely untraceable. It'll be big news by tomorrow.' Essa grimaced: 'But we cannot do it again, and I'm worried the men are becoming restless.'

'Wife, do not fear. Allah is watching over us. It will not be long now.' Al-Yussuv kissed the woman on her bared forehead and ran a hand through her cropped black hair. 'I loved your hair, dearest one.'

She smiled. 'I did not want to risk tripping on it when the action starts, Ilham.'

He kissed her again and then their lips met. Al-Yussuv's mobile rang. He pulled back, stood and walked over to where he had left the phone next to his commando jacket. He heard a click and then a series of bleeps. He counted them. Four. He pushed the red button and then punched in a number he had memorised. He said nothing.

A distorted voice at the other end of the line delivered one short, crisp sentence: 'Friday, nine thirty a.m. T3.' Al-Yussuv heard another click and the line went dead. Essa looked at him expectantly. 'Friday morning,' he said, feeling his hand shaking as he held the phone at his side.

CHAPTER 3

Wednesday, 7.30 a.m., 64 miles north of London

Ilham Al-Yussuv gazed through the window at the green summer fields dotted with sheep. He was alone in the train carriage, but he knew five of his men were scattered throughout the other fifteen carriages of the 5.55 a.m. express from Bradford to London's King's Cross.

Everything had been planned down to the tiniest detail. The cell had split into seven groups. The teams had all travelled, or were now travelling, to London via entirely separate routes: three by car taking different roads south, one by coach, two by train and a final team in three trucks hidden with their equipment behind crates. Al-Yussuv looked down at his tailored suit, neatly ironed shirt and Windsor-knotted tie. As Dr Omar Shalim, an orthopaedic surgeon returning from a medical conference at the Norcroft Centre, Bradford, he had drawn the cushy straw: a first-class carriage and a Louis Vuitton briefcase. He also had a large suitcase filled with weapons, gas masks, explosives and sophisticated computer equipment.

The first sign of trouble came with a slowing of the train. A shiver of anxiety shuddered through him, but he pushed it away. Trains slow down and speed up all the time, even the expresses. But then it slowed some more, jolted and went into an emergency brake. Al-Yussuv was thrown from his seat and flew across the narrow space between the rows. Cursing loudly, he landed, twisted, on the padded seat in front of him.

The train ground to a stop; the screech of metal on metal.

Al-Yussuv pulled himself upright, reached for his briefcase, unclasped the twin locks and took out his Glock. He lifted the suitcase from the rack and lowered it to the floor. Then he swung round to see his friend Haadii Fahmy coming through the doors connecting a second-class carriage with the first-class. The door opened with a hiss and Fahmy was through, an MP5K in his right hand, the barrel pointing to the floor. Al-Yussuv pulled back as Fahmy reached him.

Shouts, commands.

'Allah! This is it,' Fahmy whispered, his voice full of fear. 'How? How could they know?'

A quick burst of gunfire and the glass upper half of the door connecting the carriages shattered. Al-Yussuv glimpsed a black figure, a helmet. There was a second burst of automatic fire from the other end of the carriage, and then a terrifying silence.

Smack! The two terrorists had barely registered the canister of tear gas flying through the door to their right when a flash grenade exploded less than two metres away towards the north-facing door. As 170 decibels and a blinding light filled the carriage, Al-Yussuv's training kicked in. He threw himself to the floor, peeling off three rounds towards the nearest entrance. He glimpsed Fahmy as he stumbled forward, spinning on his heel, his 9mm sub-machine gun spraying shells. Fahmy buckled like a collapsing beach chair as his spine was shattered by a shell from a semi-automatic.

Al-Yussuv, flat on his stomach, tossed his gun forward, watching it spin along the polished floor, and raised both hands as the gas-masked firearms team charged into the carriage.

CHAPTER 4

Ealing, West London, Thursday evening

It was all over the TV and the Internet, of course. A terrorist cell busted. But the details were sketchy. Hubab Essa stared at the screen of her laptop, trying to get any scrap of information she could. One of her mobile phones trilled. It was the Nokia fitted with the highest security protocols. She snatched it up.

She had not heard the computer voice before. They had always called Ilham. But he was not here. She had no idea where he was. *Was he in heaven with his well-deserved virgins?* she mused as the voice spoke.

'The package is on schedule. No change, but you must be home to sign for it.' She understood what that meant and went to ask a question. *Did they have any news on Ilham?* But the line was dead. She stared at the blank screen and could see her reflection, a black scarf framing her narrow face, her steely eyes and tight jaw. She could not remember the last time she had laughed. 'So, I am now in command,' she said to the empty room. 'I shall not fail.' The muscles in her cheeks tightened. 'I am the Infidel's worst nightmare.'

She returned to the laptop, stabbing at keys. She was deep inside the Dark Web, but there was nothing more to learn. The British authorities had already passed on to the press as much as they were going to. If Ilham had survived, he would be in detention now and no one but the military would know anything about her husband. Central Command in Raqqa might know scraps, but comms were kept brief and strictly for essentials only. She would learn no more that way. She snapped out of it and closed the laptop lid. She had a job to do.

There came a quiet tap at the door.

'Yes.'

A young man appeared at the opening. It was her seventeen-year-old cousin, Nadir Abdallah. He was a kid, his beard patchy.

'Nadir,' Essa said. 'Come.'

He gave his elder relative a small bow and entered, closing the door behind him.

'What is it?' Essa asked. 'You look worried.'

The boy couldn't meet her eyes.

'Look me in the face, Nadir. What's wrong?'

Nadir raised his eyes, and without his needing to utter a word Essa could see what was troubling him. 'You are afraid?'

He nodded and lowered his eyes again.

'Look at me, Nadir. It is natural to be afraid. We are all afraid. But Allah gives us strength. You do love Allah, don't you, Nadir?'

'Of course, cousin. Of course I do.' He looked genuinely shocked.

'And the Infidel?'

'The Infidel must die. And I will follow you to victory tomorrow.'

'That is good.'

'I cannot sleep, cousin. I want to serve Allah and I know I shall gladly die for Islam. It is just . . .'

'You are afraid of death?'

Nadir said nothing, looked at his palms. 'I hate myself for my fear, but yes, cousin, I am. I'm afraid to die.'

'But you shall go to heaven. Your name will live for ever. You will be a martyr and you will kill many before you die. It will be a moment to make your mother proud, our whole family proud.'

He produced a strained smile. Hubab Essa stood. 'Come here, Nadir. Give your cousin a hug.'

He put his arms around his cousin's muscular, hard body. She held his shoulders. 'Now, Nadir. I have just received final confirmation that the mission is to go ahead as planned in spite of . . .'

Nadir looked at her gravely.

'I have a small but very important job for you tonight.'

They sat and Essa explained; then she watched the door close behind the kid. As it clicked shut, she picked up a second mobile and pressed a single digit. She could hear it ring in a room upstairs before the soft voice of Zahoor Ashmina, her closest lieutenant, came through the speaker. 'I need you to do something for me,' she said.

CHAPTER 5

NADIR ABDALLAH STOOD AT the back entrance to the terraced house. A small garden strewn with rubbish stretched to a gate in the wooden fence. He moved quickly, unlatched the gate with shaking fingers and dashed into the dark alleyway running behind the scruffy houses. A left, a right; keeping to the shadows, he was out on the quiet street.

He swerved into the street with a small parcel under his right arm. His instructions from Essa were clear. He needed to drop the parcel in a waste bin outside a grocer's shop on the main road. He turned down another narrow lane, through puddles. Muddy water splashed up his trouser legs, but he didn't care at all. Then he was out on another, bigger street that led to Western Avenue, thirty metres ahead.

Single-focused, Nadir stepped from the pavement onto the tarmac without paying any attention to anything around him. He believed that this part of the mission was everything. Essa had impressed upon him the importance of the parcel and the drop.

An old black Ford came round the corner, its lights off. It accelerated along the short road. Nadir was so lost in his own world he only heard the car when it was five yards from him. The headlights came on – full beam – a blinding light. Nadir froze, like a rabbit. Then some sort of survival instinct booted up and with a great burst of energy, he leapt forward. But it was too late, far too late. The car hit him square on at forty miles per hour.

Nadir left the ground, slid up the bonnet and the windscreen like a ski jumper in reverse. He spun round a metre above the car and smacked onto the road with a loud, hollow crunch.

His former colleague, Zahoor Ashmina, tightened his fingers on the wheel and kept driving. Nadir was dead before the Ford reached the end of the street. The car screeched around the corner and Ashmina returned to the house via an indirect route.

CHAPTER 6

'Black' Detention Centre, North-west London, Friday, 8.44 a.m.

'The fucker won't break!' SAS officer Colonel Jack Stewart hissed. 'Thirty-five hours, and nothing.' He and Captain Nigel Grant were in the corridor. Stewart glared at the door in front of him. 'I'm not sure I could hold out that long. You have to give the bastard credit.'

Behind the door, a long, narrow room; low ceiling, powerful fluorescent strip lights, a metal floor streaked with blood. In the centre of the room, a table. At one end, a trough filled with water. Beside the trough on the metal floor lay a pile of towels and next to this, a bucket half-filled with freezing-cold water. A hosepipe ran from a tap inserted into one of the room's shorter walls.

On the table lay Ilham Al-Yussuv, his body covered with bruises and lacerations. His blood had pooled under him and dripped from the table to the floor. Al-Yussuv was barely conscious. He had no idea where he was or how long he had been here. All he knew was a world of pain, agonies he had never imagined possible. He'd been cut, beaten, burned and waterboarded. But he would say nothing. He had told them his name but no more, not a clue, not a hint. The Infidel would never break him. He would never betray Allah. *Allahu Akbar! Allahu Akbar!*

All the British had was what Al-Yussuv had been carrying with him when he was caught on the train: a suitcase full of weapons, explosives and other equipment; and an expensive briefcase which contained two things – a plastic box holding feta-and-tomato sandwiches and a copy of the Quran. The book had been analysed by intelligence officers trained to unravel hidden coded messages, but they had drawn a complete blank.

Outside in the corridor, Captain Nigel Grant turned his back to the door. 'All our intel says something will happen today, this morning. But where? The clock is ticking, sir.'

'Really, Captain? You're a damn sage, you know that?'

A heavy silence. For the colonel it was only the second time he had been ordered to use illegal methods to break a prisoner; for Grant, it was a first. They hated it, they were not animals. But the intel was clear. This was a big one. Thousands of lives might be at stake, so the gloves were off.

From far off they could hear an electronic hum, a generator in Classroom Block D. The building, the two men knew, was a derelict school, and the military had kept the old names from the fifties when kids had run along these corridors. The room in which Al-Yussuv lay had perhaps held a geography class.

'Right. We focus on this shit's buddy, the young guy. Miah Ahmadi.'

'He's a nothing, sir,' Grant replied. 'Al-Yussuv knows the entire plan, whatever that is. Ahmadi is just suicide-bomb fodder.'

'Got any better ideas, Captain? As you so wisely pointed out, we're running out of time. Anything will help, any clue. Al-Yussuv will die before he says a word. He's a fucking robot.'

CHAPTER 7

THE KID *WAS* A nobody. That much Captain Grant had right. But he was tough: brainwashing and religious zealotry tended to have that effect on people. He had his god to protect him. He knew he would die a martyr. He would go to heaven.

Miah Ahmadi's family were from Yemen, but had moved over to England in the seventies. His father worked at a toy factory near their home on Oak Lane, in the Bradford suburb of Allerton, making trinkets for Christian bastards and Jew-spawn. Miah had turned nineteen last April. He hated his parents. They were, he believed, 'Slaves of the Infidel' and he had walked out on them the day he finished school. For two years, he had lived at the mosque on Thornbury Road.

The SAS officers entered the room. Ahmadi lay on a similar table to the one on which Al-Yussuv had endured so much. Ahmadi had been waterboarded, too. The paraphernalia lay all around.

The colonel leaned over the boy. 'Patience running low, Miah,' he said. The boy felt the man's hot breath.

'Time to talk,' Captain Grant added. He was leaning against the wall, arms folded across his broad chest.

'I don't know nothing,' the youth croaked, his Yorkshire accent thick as black pudding. His mouth was so dry he could barely form whole words.

'Nothing? Sure about that, Miah?'

'You got nothin' from—' He stopped short. *Give no information*, he had been taught. *Loose talk is deadly.*

He felt proud of himself. He was a real soldier of Allah. They had his weapons and his bomb vest, and these filthy animals, these scum, had waterboarded him, cut him, beaten him, yet still he had said nothing apart from his name.

Grant pulled away from the wall and helped the colonel tighten the leather straps holding Ahmadi's feet and hands to the table.

What was happening now? the kid thought. *What now?* He turned to face Grant, but the soldier grabbed him, held his head still and Ahmadi felt a strap being laid over his forehead. He just caught a glimpse of a rack of machines to one side of the bed. Then a wire touched his cheek and he felt Captain Grant fix something to the head strap. He could not see him, but the boy felt the other man moving, and then cold air as his trousers were ripped open. Something brushed his scrotum and then came a bolt of pain as a clamp was tightened.

'Start at one hundred volts,' Jack Stewart said. Grant threw the switch and Ahmadi convulsed, his back arching. His screams reverberated around the room.

'Speak, Miah. Tell us.'

The kid said nothing. Sweat ran down his face and mingled with his tears. He shook his head.

'One-fifty,' Stewart said.

The switch was snapped down again.

'Noooo!' Ahmadi screamed.

'Speak.'

'Noooo!'

Stewart nodded to Grant. He adjusted a dial on the side of the machine at the top of the rack and electricity surged through Ahmadi's frail body. The screams were almost unbearable. Almost.

'I'll . . .'

'Yes?' It was Grant. He *really* wanted this to end.

'Allah, help me,' Miah whispered.

Grant leaned forward.

'Church . . .' the boy groaned.

'Churchill Airport?' Colonel Stewart snapped.

Ahmadi produced the tiniest nod and closed his eyes.

'Where in the airport?

Ahmadi tried to resist, shook his head again.

'Pump it up to two hundred,' Stewart ordered.

'But that'll—'

'Do it.'

'Wait. Please . . . wait,' the boy sobbed, his eyes half-open.

'You have three seconds,' Stewart spat, his face an inch from the boy's. 'Three . . . two . . .'

'Four. Terminal Four.'

Ahmadi's facial muscles froze, his eyes wide open. 'Terminal Four, Churchill Airport.'

CHAPTER 8

SWEAT DRIPPED DOWN MUHAMMAD Girgrah's face and he hastily wiped it away. Passing through security, his guts were doing somersaults. He flashed his pass at the guard and pushed the metal-framed food cart through the scanner. The security guard gave Muhammad a brief smile. They'd talked before, shot the breeze, grouched about their wives and lives over a cigarette.

Through the scanner, Muhammad peeled off left along a corridor away from the route to the restaurant. Shaking still, his mouth bone dry, he headed straight to Arrivals and passed under a roller door that had been raised and fixed in place over a ramp leading to double doors. Inside, he saw signs overhead, arrows to 'Gates 1–9', 'Gates 10–23'; 'WAY OUT'; 'TOILETS', solid figures of a man and a woman. He reached Gate 0, an out-of-the-way spot where even the security-camera footage was barely glanced at. He could feel his heart pounding.

It was quiet. He saw a chef in a striped apron with a hat clasped in his hand as he dashed towards the kitchens a long way back. Then he was in the open, a wide but empty expanse, huge windows opening out to the tarmac. The nearest plane was far off at the regular gates in the main hubs. He hung another left and backed up to a door, the cart in front of him. A small plastic sign on the door read: 'STAFF ONLY'.

He flicked on the light switch and a fluorescent strip beat on and off, then splashed around a sickly lemon light. One end of the room was filled with boxes. A chair had been placed in front of them. A tall man with a beard down to his waist was seated in the chair. He was wearing a white robe and conical hat, a thick leather belt and sandals – a costume worn over two thousand years ago by the elite warriors of the ancient Mede tribe.

Muhammad was startled, but pulled himself together, bowed and pulled the cart into the room. He started to unload it as the man watched him silently. With all the boxes piled on the floor, Muhammad dismantled the frame, stood the parts against the wall, took one of the struts, popped the square metal cap from the end and slipped his fingers carefully into the tube. He gingerly withdrew a length of glistening steel.

The tall man stood, towering over Muhammad; he was at least six foot six with a physique like a young Arnold Schwarzenegger. His hair hung in long ringlets from the base of the conical hat, and his dark eyes shrouded by thick black brows were unreadable. He removed a leather cylinder from a pocket in his robe and held out his other hand for Muhammad to pass him the length of metal.

The giant fitted the leather tube to the end of the shiny blade and twisted it. A satisfying click. 'Good, good,' he said, his voice a rich baritone. He raised the slender length of metal and slashed the air, making Mohammed jump back in terror. The man traced a finger along the edge of the blade, watching a trickle of blood slide down onto his palm. 'Excellent!'

CHAPTER 9

THE LEARJET NUDGED FORWARD ready to dock, its engines beginning to quieten, when suddenly the sound of the twin Honeywell turbines grew louder and shriller as the jet quickly backed away from the gate.

Saudi Prince Adil al-Salhi jolted forward in his seat and glared at his head of security, Dirar Radi.

Radi raised his hands. 'Nothing to worry about, my Prince.' He held a hand to his earpiece, nodded and produced a relaxed smile. 'Change of gate, that's all. MI5 will meet us at another. It is not far. They wanted a last-minute change . . . For our safety!' He gave his boss a look of disdain.

Prince Adil al-Salhi had every reason to be jumpy. He was on the run, a fugitive from his own family. Intelligent, with a naturally gentle character, Adil had been educated at Brasenose College, Oxford, where he had been 'de-radicalised'. He had grown to hate his government, the relentless cruelty of the Saudi regime; and he had struck a deal with British intelligence – a thorough debriefing, everything he knew about his evil uncles and their worthless minions in exchange for a cast-iron, secure new identity and round-the-clock protection.

Three minutes later, the plane skirted the edges of Terminal 3 and edged into Gate 0. Prince Adil al-Salhi gazed at the grey stone, glass and steel as Dirar Radi stood and removed a metal briefcase from a locked compartment towards the rear of the plane.

Radi, his Glock producing a bulge in his buttoned-up Armani suit jacket, led the way, followed by the prince in his white robe and keffiyeh, the traditional Saudi headdress. Behind them strode two more guards, AK-47s at their hips.

CHAPTER 10

HUBAB ESSA'S TEAM WAS the first to arrive and meet up. They had spread out in ones and twos and were now gathered in a long-stay car park on Eastern Perimeter Road close to Terminal 3.

'Group Green, status,' Essa said quietly into her secure mobile as she punched key 5. Some static, then Vafi Akel's voice replied: 'In position.' She clicked off and called each commander of the other five surviving groups. They had each taken up position around Terminal 3. They were ready.

Essa checked her watch: 9.14. Via her modified phone, she sent a signal to each of the groups. A signal that meant move to Stage 4, the penultimate step in the opening phase of the operation. She then set off for the lifts, pulling her suitcase behind her. A minute later, two others in her group, brothers Parizad and Cemal, walked to the lifts on the far side of the car park, each dragging two cases and carrying a large shoulder bag. Jaad followed Essa ninety seconds later, and Nizam after him. Finally, the sixth member of Group Red, Ruhi, carrying a large backpack and two smaller shoulder bags, took the stairs. By 9.26, they were all in the arrivals hall of Terminal 3. Another sixty seconds passed as they each converged on the gents' toilets in the corner furthest from the main concourse.

Essa was the last to arrive. She closed the door to the outside and strode into the clinical white room lined with urinals. The place stank of bleach. Two businessmen in suits stood close to the basins, a wide mirror behind them, their hands on their heads. Their faces were as white as cooked albumen. Essa noticed with satisfaction that one of the men had pissed his pants; the crotch of his smart suit was sodden and dark.

Without a word, Essa pulled her Glock from her jacket, screwed on a silencer and shot the executives in the head. They collapsed in two bloody heaps.

They all heard a sound from one of the cubicles. Essa pumped the door with five shots in quick succession; a body fell to the floor and a stream of blood ran from under the shattered door.

Essa checked her watch: 9.28.

'Two minutes,' she snapped, and the six of them started to unpack the cases and bags.

CHAPTER 11

CHAZ AND I HAVE this ritual. It goes back six years now, since my divorce. Chaz? He's a career bachelor. We meet once a year at JFK or Churchill and catch a cheap flight to a sunny holiday destination. One year it was Tijuana, another it was Majorca, last year Florida. And that's why I had been racing along the M4. I was running late for the prearranged meet-up with Chaz, fresh off his Virgin Atlantic flight from Kennedy. I had the tickets for our flight to Athens and from there we planned to catch a ferry from Piraeus to the Greek island of Mykonos. Two weeks of sun, women, beer and relaxation – just what we needed. I had Skyped Chaz the day before and he'd looked completely wrung out.

I checked in my bag. The pretty young woman at the desk eyed my passport. 'Welcome, Captain Bates.'

That always brought a smile to my lips. I had been discharged from the army 'without honour', but as an act of defiance I kept my title in my passport. It was a shame I had to get a fresh one soon and would lose the 'Captain'. But that was the least of it. Thanks to the 'without honour', the best job I could get was as a security guard for G4S. Maybe you can get a sense of why 'wifey' left, taking my beloved son Tommy with her. I was now working sixty hours a week to pay alimony and save for one holiday a year.

'Anything flammable in the bag? You packed it yourself?' the check-in assistant asked.

'No. Yes.' Questions answered and boarding gate circled in pen, I strode towards Arrivals to wait for Chaz. I checked the board and saw the 9.18 from JFK had just landed. Chaz would soon be coming through and we would pump hands, smack each other on the back and head for the connecting flight.

It was a great arrangement. We lived on different continents but always had a cool two weeks a year together. The only potential problem was that we had pretty much the same taste in women, so on holiday it was sometimes a race to the start line. Apart from women, Chaz and I had something else in common. He had saved my life and I his. I'm ex-SAS and Chaz was a Delta Force captain who was not just badass; he has a brain and is a cyber-combat expert. Back in 2009, Chaz had pulled me from the wreck of a landmined Foxhound Protected Mobility Vehicle in Iraq. A year later, on a UK/US joint black ops mission, I'd saved Chaz when he came within a flea's breath of gagging on a sniper's bullet.

I ran along the carpet, dodged a vehicle driven by a young guy wearing a yellow vest transporting an old couple. Chaz was exiting as I rocked up. He gave me his best bear hug, and with grins a mile wide, we were off, heading back the way I had come.

'You look great, man,' Chaz said, eyeing me up and down. 'Good gym?'

'So-so. Too pricey.'

'And how's Tommy?'

'He's cool. Ten next month. I wish I could see more of him, but it's strictly one weekend in three.'

We passed along the main corridor. Other passengers dashed towards and past us. It was peak time, holiday season, a week after the schools had finished for the long summer holiday. It didn't get crazier than this.

Another oldies' express was heading straight for us. I pulled Chaz out of the way and saw a narrower, less crowded passage to my right. 'We can get duty-free nearer the gate,' I said.

'And you have got my boarding pass for the Greek flight?'

'You'll never forgive me that one time, will you?'

'Nope.'

'I know a quick back way to Departures.' I hung a left and then another right between a storeroom and a sweetshop. Chaz had just a belt-bag; his suitcase would be in baggage handling.

It was oddly quiet here.

'You've managed to get us lost, haven't you, Einstein?' Chaz said.

'No. I'm sure this is right.'

Chaz checked his watch. 'Cutting it fine, buddy. Let's go back, take the regular route, yeah?'

I nodded. 'Guess.'

That's when we got the first shock.

CHAPTER 12

'HOLY FUCK!' I EXCLAIMED. The words just spilled out. I froze and felt Chaz pull up beside me.

I'd had guns pointed at me more times than I cared to remember, but never here, in England, at Churchill Airport, Terminal 3. A man in an Armani suit was standing between two Arabs in white robes who were brandishing AK-47s.

One of the robed guys shrieked, and I thought: *This is it. We're dead.* But then the dude in the suit dropped a metal briefcase between his feet and raised his gun in both hands.

'Get your hands up,' said the guy in the suit.

Chaz was as startled as me, and for a crazy second, neither of us moved.

'Get your fucking hands up or you are both dead!' Armani-man had a thick Middle Eastern accent swamping the English words. Chaz and I put our hands up.

Then it was the wall. Smack. My nose up against the plaster. I could hear Chaz's heavy breath beside me. He and I knew better than to argue. We were unarmed and had obviously stumbled into something we really shouldn't have stumbled into. I felt the swish of a robe as I was patted down; a hand ran down each leg, then came a barked Arabic word: '*Wadh*.' Clear.

We heard footsteps and a fresh voice: 'Gentlemen. Please, calm down. Release them.'

I felt myself spun round and I glanced at Chaz. He looked like he was about to explode. New Yorkers, especially ex-Delta Force New Yorkers, don't like to be shoved around any more than the next man.

'Apologies,' the new arrival said. He wore a Savile Row suit and black Oxfords polished to perfection. I clocked the old Beretta in his right hand. It was the same gun packed by my favourite Bond, Sean Connery. The guy oozed Her Majesty's Secret Intelligence Service – I had met a few of his type before. Behind him stood another man in a robe and a keffiyeh. He was tall and delicately built and looked like a Saudi prince. 'You appear to have lost your way, gentlemen,' Mr MI5 said. He looked almost amused. I liked him.

'Guess, so,' Chaz said. He was really pissed off, I could tell.

'I think you'll find the public areas are that way,' the English guy replied and pointed to our left. 'We're headed thataway.'

We stood watching for a second, and I remember thinking how neither of us could see any funny side to it, but perhaps we would later, over a beer. That's when I saw the shadow, and before anyone else could move, I was sprinting towards the group without a thought for what I was actually doing.

CHAPTER 13

THE SHADOW MORPHED INTO a white-robed figure in a conical hat. A massive guy. And he was wielding a huge curved sword.

In a fraction of a second, I was past the security guards and the two men in suits. I registered the prince in my periphery, his face blank; he hadn't yet noticed anything wrong. I sensed Chaz immediately behind me. And then I was there. I swung a leg and it made contact with the sword hand of the giant. My Doc Marten caught the guy's ulna collateral ligament and smashed his styloid processes. I'd learned the anatomical terms in Special Forces training. It was a long time ago, but it had stuck and I knew the bastard would never swing another sword.

The sabre slipped from the man's hand and flew, spinning end over end, to land almost silently on the beige carpet a few yards to his right. I followed through without drawing breath. The prince's guards were still frozen as I swung a fist into the big man's face and heard a satisfyingly loud crack. That was his jaw fracturing.

I saw Chaz then. He had anticipated my moves with professional precision and had taken two steps to his left. As my fist pulled back from the giant's shattered face, Chaz landed a heavy boot into the guy's solar plexus and he was down, a huge amoeba on the floor.

The prince's guards finally moved. The two with the AK-47s stepped inwards, closing ranks and shielding the Saudi royal. The leader of the prince's guard sprang forward, his pistol at a steep angle pointed directly at the swordsman's head.

'Stop, Dirar!' the British agent said and leapt to the guard's side. 'No shooting.'

The guard turned to the MI5 escort as a trickle of sweat wove a jagged path down his cheek. He looked confused.

'Get him up,' the British guy snapped and the white-robed guards dashed forward. They took an arm each, pulled his hands back behind him and held the huge attacker between them.

It had all happened in less than six seconds.

The big guy had lost his hat in the fight and his curled hair was a mess. He was built like a tank. I'm six four and he was taller than me. He was conscious and wanted to speak; I saw his mouth move, but all that came out was blood and an unintelligible series of groans. He wouldn't form real words again for a long time, I thought.

The MI5 agent pulled out his mobile phone. 'Delta Three. We have met with resistance.' A pause. 'Affirmative.' He pocketed the phone and said to the guard: 'Two of my men will be here in ninety seconds.'

The prince turned to Chaz and me and dipped his head. 'I am Prince Adil al-Salhi and this is the head of my guard, Dirar Radi. You saved my life. I am in your debt.'

'All in a day's work,' I quipped, and Prince Adil smiled.

'I shall ensure you are rewarded.' He turned to Chaz and then back to me.

'That won't be necessary,' I said and heard Chaz sigh. I gave him a dirty look.

'I'm guessing ex-military,' the MI5 agent said, stepping up beside the prince.

'Something like that,' Chaz said.

'I too am grateful. Apologies again for the earlier mistake.'

'What will happen to him?' Chaz asked, flicking a glance at the swordsman dangling between the robed guards.

'Oh, I wouldn't worry about him, gentlemen.' The agent took in Chaz and me, then turned with a guiding hand on the prince's arm. The prince glanced round and beamed at us.

That's when the shit really hit the fan.

CHAPTER 14

THE ROBED GUARDS HAD let go of their AK-47s and they hung at their sides on leather shoulder straps. The MI5 guy, Delta 3, was re-holstering his Beretta and the lead guard in the suit, Dirar Radi, had stepped a couple of paces forward away from us as Chaz and I had started to turn. Then Radi dropped his briefcase and lifted his pistol.

Chaz and I hit the floor simultaneously. Radi began firing his Glock, the silencer producing a *phat, phat, phat* as the shells spat from the end of the barrel and found targets. We pulled up, crouched low and dashed out of the gunman's sight. We were on opposite sides of the causeway; I was behind a pillar, while Chaz had ducked behind a line of chairs. He wasn't that safe there and he knew it. He ran again, to a column mirroring mine across the corridor.

I couldn't see all of the scene, but I didn't want to risk having my head blown off for a better view. Radi hit the MI5 agent first. He was the biggest threat. I saw a Glock shell smash into the man's forehead and he was dead before he hit the floor.

The prince was petrified and utterly confounded. His hands shot up as he stared at his trusted employee, a man he had considered a friend, a friend who had volunteered to go with him into hiding and exile. He looked from Radi's face to the gun in the man's hand. The traitor fired three shots into the prince's chest, blowing great holes out of his back. I felt a surge of fury rush through me. *What the fuck was going on?* I shot a glance over to Chaz. I had no way of telling how much he had seen from his position.

One of the guards in white robes managed to reach his assault rifle. The swordsman tipped forwards, just keeping his balance, grabbed the AK-47 with his one good hand and yanked it. The second guard ducked and went for his weapon. Radi fired at him, missed, and a pair of bullets hit the edge of the column two inches from my nose. I pulled back, heard the *rat-tat-tat* of a Kalashnikov's shells and dared to peep at the scene. The swordsman had shot a guard with his own gun. The second guard had gone down on one knee and had his AK-47 in both hands. He was raising it when Radi shot him.

I felt stomach acid burning in my throat. We were defenceless and something told me we wouldn't be popular with Radi, even less so with the injured swordsman we had taken down. I saw Chaz again, and this time he was looking across at me. He flicked a glance to the causeway behind us indicating that our best hope was to make a dash for it away from the two killers. I knew we had little choice, but it was a dangerous move. I really didn't fancy our chances.

But then things got even stranger.

CHAPTER 15

THE BIG GUY, WITH the guard's AK-47 in his one good hand, the strap over his healthy shoulder, was peering our way. He was a mess, but a very dangerous mess with the assault rifle between him and us. And he had backup, the treacherous bastard, Dirar Radi – I could barely see him behind the swordsman's sheer bulk.

I didn't register the pops, just saw the swordsman straighten, adding another couple of inches to his giant frame. The red stain took a second to show in the fabric of his robe. But then it spread fast. He turned towards Radi with the AK-47 level. Radi fired twice more, head shots that brought the giant to his knees. Like a felled elephant, he just tipped forward, face first, and slammed to the ground.

I saw movement on the floor. It was one of the robed guards; the one the swordsman had shot. He rolled over, found his buddy's gun and reached for the trigger. Radi caught the movement in his peripheral vision and brought his gun down, fired, and the guard died before he could loose a round.

Radi saw me. He had straightened and lifted the gun. I had lost count of the shots he'd fired. He was using a Glock 19. It carried fifteen shells. How many had he peeled off? At least a dozen. I couldn't risk it. Besides, he might have replaced the cartridge when I wasn't looking; he could even have had a second gun.

I clocked Chaz move and Radi shift position. He turned his pistol towards my friend and pulled the trigger. Nothing happened. He was out. But the bastard was also good, a real pro. He had one of the AK-47s in his hands before Chaz or I could even decide what to do. Straightening, Radi sprayed the column I was behind and then pumped more shells Chaz's way.

I could just see him now through a narrow gap between the column and the wall. His gun was pointed at us as he crouched. He grasped the handle of the briefcase he had dropped and started to back up. Reaching a bend in the causeway, he swept the path ahead with the Kalashnikov, spun on his heel and sprinted away.

I left it a few seconds and then pulled out from behind the column, every nerve fired up, every sense 100 per cent alert.

We reached the scene of carnage. They were all dead. The carpet was soaked with blood, the bodies twisted and contorted like something from a horror movie.

I heard a voice. Chaz caught it at the same moment. He stepped forward, crouched and lifted the MI5 agent's phone. 'Delta Three. Delta Three. Respond.'

Chaz lifted the phone. 'Hi, buddy.'

Silence at the other end for two beats. 'Who's this?'

'Delta Three is dead.'

'Who is this?'

'Oh, fuck!' Chaz handed the phone to me. 'You speak English. Talk to 'em!'

I took the phone. 'There's been an attack. Everyone here's been killed – Prince al-Salhi, his guards, your man.'

Silence again. I saw Chaz pick up Delta 3's Beretta and walk over to the wall. There was a glass-fronted box. I could just make out a large round red button inside. Chaz smashed the glass with the handle of the pistol and leaned on the button. A light at the top of the box lit up crimson and a wailing sound reverberated along the causeway. It was a general panic button. The siren and more lights would be going off all over the airport.

'What the hell are you talking about?' came a voice from the end of the line. 'What's that alarm?'

I pulled the phone from my ear, switched it off and tossed it to the floor.

'Delta Three's buddies will be here in a few seconds,' Chaz said, pacing quickly back towards me. 'I really don't wanna be caught here with guns in our hands.'

'Me neither. I've been looking forward to Mykonos all year.'

I pocketed a Glock and then we were off, running at breakneck speed the way Radi had gone, the sirens blaring all around us.

CHAPTER 16

DIRAR RADI BOLTED ALONG the corridor, spinning every dozen steps and sweeping his gun. Things were not going to plan, but he would pull it back together. *Fuck those arseholes*, he thought. *Who could have imagined running into a couple of shit-kicking ex-military?* It was a test from Allah, he was sure of it.

It should have been easy. The warrior, Qanni – how many strong, enemy soldiers had the oaf slain? His had not been a tough job. He was just to rush out and behead the prince. What could have been simpler? But no. What was it the Infidel said? *The best-laid plans of mice and men . . .*

He slowed and hid his weapon as he approached a service lift. He knew the code; it changed each day. He tapped it in. A few moments later, the doors opened onto B3, the lowest level.

He crept out. No one around. If all else had gone according to the carefully worked-out plans then the team should be in place down here. Radi pulled up with his back to the wall, his gun in his right hand, briefcase in his left. He took a deep breath, then ran, fast, along the concrete corridor, the rubber soles of his shoes cushioning his footfall. Approaching the corner, he slowed and pulled back again.

He ran to the opposite wall, swinging his gun to cover the corridor ahead. A dead man lay propped up against the left wall. Radi slipped past him. He reached a left turn. He could hear sounds ahead – an electric crackle and the churning low beat of a set of gigantic boilers. Along with the rest of his team, he had studied the schematics, talked it all through with recon who had been here weeks ago, and he had rehearsed the mission. He suddenly felt a surge of confidence. Allah was with him. Allah was with this mission. They could not fail.

Ahead, a pair of doors. He slunk between them. Another body. An airport security officer in a blue uniform lay on his back, motionless.

From the schematics, Radi knew this was the boiler room, a vast space packed with gigantic tanks and cylinders, machinery, massive pipes and grinding pumps. It reminded him of a film about the *Titanic* he had seen as a kid. It looked like the engine room of a gargantuan ship. The place stank of oil and grease. He pressed on, knowing exactly where he was going. He hung a left, then a right, slowed and approached the rendezvous point.

They saw him first – his three lieutenants – Lutfullah, Jaan and Pir. Jaan had his gun thrust forward as Radi emerged from a dark, narrow gangway between boilers. Recognising his leader, he lowered his M1 Garand.

Radi stepped forward briskly. No time for pleasantries, just a nod. 'Has it gone smoothly?' he asked. 'I was delayed. But have it.' He lifted the briefcase.

'We're ready,' Pir replied. 'Just waiting for this . . .'

Radi gave him a nasty look.

'Once we have the agent, it will take no more than thirty minutes to prepare,' Pir added quickly.

Radi pocketed his weapon, lowered the case to the floor, spun the small barrels of the combo lock and flicked open the catches. The four men gazed down at the canister containing a colourless liquid. 'The traitor prince had no idea I had the final piece of our jigsaw on his plane.' Radi lifted the cylinder from the foam padding of the case. 'Behold. Soman, a nerve agent twice as toxic as sarin and far faster-acting. Enough to wipe out a small city in minutes. And we are positioned at the epicentre of a small city, my friends. Churchill Airport.'

CHAPTER 17

'LADIES AND GENTLEMEN,' THE voice came over the PA. 'We would ask you to please remain calm. There has been an incident far from the main concourses. The alarm is an automatic precaution. Please remain where you are. Repeat: please remain where you are.' The message began again on auto-repeat.

Chaz and I reached the edge of the sectioned-off private jet area and saw no one. Radi had vanished.

'Need to alert security,' Chaz said as we paused for a second. 'Christ only knows what he had in that case.'

'Agreed.' I hitched my backpack into a more comfortable position and we sped off towards the public areas where all routes led to the main arrivals hub. We took a right and found a bank of service lifts.

'Any idea where security HQ would be?' Chaz asked.

I shrugged and then saw a map on the wall across from the lifts. 'I'd guess it would be on the periphery. Let's hope it's this end of the terminal.'

We studied the map for a few seconds and at the same moment we spotted the symbol for the security headquarters. 'Not far. Up one level.'

We moved fast and reached Level 1. My heart was racing and I suspected that Chaz was feeling pretty crap after a transatlantic flight. He had left the military soon after me, but had done a whole lot better for himself. He had his own security consultancy firm. I would have been over the pond like a shot to work for him if it wasn't for my son Tommy.

We hit the first public area on Level 1 and sensed the fear immediately. It was so heavy in the air you could almost smell it. Everyone has the jitters in airports. It lurks just beneath the surface. It's either nerves about flying, the fear of authority pinning you like a bug to flypaper at security, or the possibility of a terror attack. People feel vulnerable in airports, on their guard.

The same warning message spilled again from the PA. The alarms stopped ringing and with a knee-jerk reaction people clammed up immediately. The quiet was eerie, the spell only broken when a baby suddenly started to cry.

There was a large crowd in Arrivals. Chaz and I could see it from a mezzanine level on the landside of passport control and baggage collection. Through a wall of glass we saw people in groups and small family units milling around.

'Come on,' I said. 'It's up ahead, on this floor – left then right.'

We reached the corner and almost smashed into two security guards. They had their guns drawn, big Walther P99s. The younger of the two looked terrified. They stopped us.

'What the . . .?' the older guard yelled. He had a Dublin accent thick as Irish mud.

'The incident happened at Gate Zero. That way,' Chaz said.

'And you know this how?' A voice was coming over the guard's radio, addressing him as O'Leary, but he ignored it.

'We were there,' I said. I reached for my passport. The young guard panicked and lifted his gun.

'Whoa!' Chaz exclaimed. 'Chill, buddy.'

O'Leary put his hand on the kid's gun, lowered it and gave him a condescending look.

'I think you gentlemen should come with us, back this way.'

'O'Leary. Where are you?' The Irish guard pushed down a button on the radio at his shoulder. 'Control. Me and Silver have two suspects in Causeway Five.'

'We're not suspects!' I snapped. 'There was a guy. Arab. He was escorting a VIP at Gate Zero.' I nodded the way we had come. 'He had a case. He killed everyone.'

'And you got away?'

I reached for my passport again. 'If you would just . . .'

I removed the document and handed it over. The young guard shifted his gaze between Chaz and me. He was perspiring: the underarms of his shirt were wet and darkened with sweat. I thought he was going to piss himself at any moment, and that made me nervous: he had a gun.

O'Leary gazed at my passport. 'Captain Matthew Bates.'

'Ex-SAS,' I said. It was not something I advertised, but I thought on this occasion it might be useful.

O'Leary tried not to look impressed.

'This is my friend, Chaz Shoeman. Just in from JFK.'

O'Leary turned to Chaz. 'Military too, I suppose?' He clocked my friend's ripped physique.

Chaz just nodded.

'How do we know you're not terrorists?' the kid said, beads of perspiration visible on his forehead.

'You don't,' Chaz shot back. 'But every second we waste here on this shit, a heavily armed Middle Eastern guy with a briefcase is closer to achieving whatever it is he has planned.'

'O'Leary?' the voice over his radio repeated.

'Yeah, yeah. OK, Spencer! Feck! I'm on my way back to the office.' He clicked off the radio. 'Where you guys headed?' O'Leary gave me a hard look.

'To try to stop the killer.'

The young guard's radio burst into life. 'Silver. Get your arse to check-in. Is O'Leary still with you?'

'I am,' O'Leary responded wearily. He shook his head and looked from me to Chaz. 'A week from retirement, one feckin' week and this feckin' happens! Come on. You heard the man. You're spoiling for a fight, so let's get to check-in.'

CHAPTER 18

IT WASN'T FAR BACK to the service lift. O'Leary led the way and made sure we ran along between him and Silver, who had his gun raised and ready the whole way. The doors opened and Silver punched in the code. O'Leary stabbed 'G' for the ground floor.

The doors opened onto a narrow corridor. A few feet ahead stood a massive glass window rising up to Departures and the level we'd just left. We could see the outside beyond the glass, the Economy drop-off and a pedestrian walkway to the nearest car park.

Two feet outside the lift we were caught up in a crazy rush of people, a dozen passengers stampeding past us. I spun round as a woman hurtled towards me, screaming. I hadn't seen anyone that scared since Afghanistan. I stepped into her path and grabbed her shoulders. 'What's happened?' I asked as calmly as I could.

She stared at me, her eyes huge, put her hand to her mouth as though she was about to vomit, pulled back with surprising strength and darted away heading to the outside, the south side of the building.

I caught sight of a younger woman. She'd dropped her bag and was spinning on her heels, left then right. 'James?' she cried, her face a mask of terror, the blood completely drained away. 'JAMES?'

I ran over and held her shoulders.

'My lad . . .' She yelled again: 'JAMES?'

Twisting round, I caught sight of a boy of about five on the other side of the glass window. He was sobbing.

'There,' I said and turned to the woman. 'Go! The door to the outside is on your right.' I nodded towards a revolving door ten metres away. She dashed off, too petrified to say a word.

We heard machine-gun fire, the crisp bang of a smoke grenade.

'This way,' O'Leary hollered close to my ear. I pulled back and saw him wave his gun towards the main check-in hall.

We slipped around the side of the lifts. More panicking passengers rushed headlong towards us. Above the noise, I could just make out the public announcement repeating the loop again. Then it stopped mid-message. Someone had evidently found the 'off' switch.

We crossed a wide stretch of hall. I drew my Glock and saw Chaz had the Beretta in his hand. We traversed the space and stopped behind a cream-painted wall squeezed between a drinks dispenser and a public Internet booth. Then O'Leary pulled away and crept to the end of the wall. He peered round the corner, and without warning stepped forward, his gun in both hands. 'Drop your weapon,' I heard him shout.

Two shots rang out and the old security guard flew through the air. He spun a half-turn and landed on his side. Two men in commando fatigues and balaclavas, each brandishing FN P90s, just about the deadliest personal defence weapons on the planet, appeared at the end of the wall. Without taking a breath, Chaz and I and the kid, Silver, all put our hands up.

'Down on your knees,' one of the men yelled. He was English and I could detect a northern accent.

We dropped. They grabbed our weapons. 'OK. Now get up,' the second guy snapped. It was definitely a northern accent, I thought: *Leeds? Manchester?*

We got to our feet. 'Make one false move and you join the old bloke. Right?'

Bradford. Definitely Bradford.

I reached the end of the wall and saw the check-in hall had become a war zone.

CHAPTER 19

SMOKE DRIFTED AROUND THE check-in desks like a North Sea fog on a winter's night. The dead had been left where they had fallen. The injured had been finished off by having their throats cut; no wasted ammo that way.

Several bodies lay on the stone floor, streaks of blood all around. One passenger was slumped over a counter and I could see from the entrance the pretty young check-in assistant who had checked my passport earlier. She had been strafed by machine-gun fire and had collapsed onto the belt that takes bags to the larger conveyor; she was jammed there, pulled back and then forward, her head banging repeatedly on the sharp edge that guides luggage.

I heard a low moan come from Silver as he took in the scene. Chaz and I stood rigid, barely able to assimilate. There must have been four hundred, maybe five hundred people in the hall, penned in by two dozen terrorists in black fatigues, some with balaclavas, some bare-faced. At each exit stood two heavily armed men, the wires and bulges of their bomb vests clearly visible.

I felt the nozzle of a gun in my back and took two steps further into the expansive open hall with its lines of check-ins each side and groups of terrified civilians.

'Stop.'

Chaz and I immediately froze. The young security guard, Silver, was pushed away to another part of the arrivals hall.

A hard prod in the back. 'Sit.'

We sat.

One of the men came round in front of us, the short muzzle of his nasty-looking FN P90 passing from Chaz to me and back again. I gazed around, only now able to fully grasp the scale of the attack. 'Fuck,' I said and glanced at Chaz.

'Shut up! No talking,' our guard commanded. 'Take off your backpack. Give it.'

I complied, no arguments from me. He could have my boxers and deodorant and shove 'em up his arse for all I cared. He flicked the gun at Chaz. 'You. Belt-bag.'

Chaz unstrapped it and tossed it on top of my pack. 'Shucks! Before I got my euros too.'

'I said shut the fuck up,' the gunman snapped, and a whole heap of crazy thoughts shot through my mind. I'd like to see if this little rat would be quite so gobby if it was just him and me, no guns, no rules.

I analysed the scene and knew Chaz was doing the same. It was a large, open space. Even with two dozen men, the attackers were stretched to keep this many people together. But then, who wanted to be the brave dead hero? The terrorists had guns and bombs; we had nothing, and most of the people here were average folks: mums and dads with their kids, students, accountants, shop-workers. I noticed a few uniforms: two security guards, bloodied and beaten, a cleaner, a flight crew. It looked like the gunmen holding the prisoners at bay were packing serious weaponry, but none of them wore bomb vests. *Makes sense*, I thought. The danger of one terrorist killing a few others if something went wrong was very real. The guys at the exits stood apart, none of their mates near them.

That's when Chaz nudged me in the ribs. I didn't move immediately, or too fast, but turned to the right. Above check-in E5A, a flat-screen TV was on. A reporter was talking to camera. It was impossible to hear what the woman was saying but there was a broad blue strip across the bottom of the screen. I could just about read the words: 'TERROR ATTACK AT CHURCHILL'. Behind the reporter stood Terminal 3, the building we were in at that very moment. The reporter was positioned at least a hundred metres to our east, past the First and Business Class drop-off points. I could make out a 'Do Not Cross' tape. Soldiers and armed police ran by with no regard for the media.

The sound of choppers broke over the TV. They were flying really low, six metres above the roof, I guessed: recon. There would be drones up there too, infrared cameras trained on the check-in hall.

I noticed that, beyond the TV screen and to the left, a video camera had been set up on a tripod. In front of it, a chair. As I stared, a woman in fatigues, a Kalashnikov strap and ammo belt crossing her jacket, lowered herself into the chair. Her hair was black as soot and cut short. She had deep stress grooves in her cheeks and a notch in her lower forehead just above her nose that would take a whole shitload of Botox to bang out. She looked like someone who rarely smiled.

At the same moment she appeared on the TV, her voice booming over the PA. I wasn't sure how they were doing it, but they had hacked into the broadcast networks. I imagined Chaz was thinking the same thing as me: *It will be on all stations simultaneously, and on the Internet.*

'My name is Hubab Essa. My men and I have captured the check-in hall of Churchill Airport, Terminal Three,' she began, her accent Bradford with a hint of what? Iraqi? Saudi? 'I have many hostages. Each exit is covered by two of my men wearing bomb vests. What are my demands?' She made a pathetic attempt at a cynical smile, but it was more rictus grin. 'No demands. There is a chemical weapon somewhere in the terminal. It will go off in' – she checked her watch – 'thirty-one minutes. This will be my only message. Have a nice day!' The screen went blank.

CHAPTER 20

I RISKED A QUICK glance at Chaz. We knew the same thing. The Arab guy with the suitcase must have been the last link in the chain. Christ only knew what chemical was being prepped. Sarin would be the most likely candidate, but there were others: something basic like mustard gas or phosgene – relatively easy to get or to synthesise, but unreliable and hard to deliver effectively. Besides, I thought, everything I had seen about this operation spelled sophistication – the advanced weapons, the TV hacking. Mustard gas or phosgene were ultra old-school. Sarin, Soman, VX, one of those three was the most likely agent. All of them were super fucking deadly, fast-acting and easy to deploy.

I moved my wrist slowly and could just read the time. It was 9.46. The bomb would go off at 10.17. I studied the immediate proximity. Our guard, a tall, wiry streak of piss, was enjoying himself. He'd pulled off his balaclava and was giving us a smug smile. I could tell he was longing to have an excuse to pump us full of P90 shells. The only time to wind up this bastard would be when Chaz and I were absolutely ready to make a move and not a second sooner. The next nearest gunman was six metres away towards the east side of the hall. He was watching a group of a dozen passengers. They were silent, petrified. He walked around them menacingly, jabbing a passenger with the muzzle of his gun, shouting at them if he heard a word or a heavy sigh of terror.

After her short message, the bitch with the cropped hair, Essa, was now striding imperiously across the shiny floor.

For a second, I thought she was coming to our little party. But then why would she? She slowed as she approached a large group, some forty civilians packed into a tight square on the floor, each cross-legged, hands on their heads. A squat, flat-faced man stood over them, his P90 at the ready, dark eyes concentrated on the hostages. He looked a bit jumpy to me. Towards the back of the block of passengers sat three tourists: mum, dad and son. The kid looked about ten, Tommy's age. As Essa approached, they each kept their eyes to the floor. I was reminded of old black-and-white war movies where the Nazi commander of the POW camp struts around and stops to inspect the captured soldiers. We'd all seen those films. Essa probably had too. She stopped beside the family.

From far off I heard a baby cry, then a few raised voices that quickly fell quiet. The baby kept crying. I heard a mother hushing – soothing, but desperate.

'Passports,' Essa said, her voice completely robotic. She kicked the father in the back. 'Passports.'

The wife handed them to her husband. He started to stand.

'Stay!

He handed them over. I could see they were American passports. *Shit!* I thought. Not a good time to be a Yank, or a Brit come to that.

Essa glanced at the passports. 'Dr Graham Steiner and Muriel Steiner travelling with' – she opened the third passport – 'little Mikey. Cute.' She tossed back the passports. 'Mikey.' Essa seemed to find it hard to say the name. 'Get up.'

The boy looked at his mum and dad. They stared back, ashen-faced.

'What do you want?' Muriel Steiner asked, her voice trembling.

'Was I talking to you, Muriel?' Essa said. 'No. I was talking to Mikey. Get up, Mikey, and come here.'

The dad nodded to the boy and the kid stood shakily. He stepped behind his parents and walked slowly towards Essa. The hall was horribly quiet.

Mikey was less than a metre from Essa and slowing. She grabbed his arm and yanked him towards her, forced him to his knees facing his mum and dad. He started to cry. Muriel Steiner went to stand, but her husband gripped her arm. I could see Dr Steiner's face. He held Essa's eyes with a look of pure hatred.

'American spawn,' Essa said, looking down at Mikey Steiner. 'One of the next generation who will bomb our people and destroy our countries. Best put to death now, I think.' She whipped her right hand round and had the Walther in her palm; the one she had used to kill the student, James Dalton. Muriel Steiner screamed as Essa pushed the gun hard into the boy's temple, making him yelp. Tears streamed down the kid's face.

Essa pulled the trigger and nothing happened. Just a click. The squat guard standing beside his commander laughed and Essa produced the magazine in her left hand. 'Oh! Forgot this,' she said coldly, and slotted it into the gun with a click.

That was when Dr Graham Steiner snapped. He sprang up, his face etched with fury, eyes ablaze. 'You fucking bitch!' he spat, and almost reached Essa before she lifted the Walther and fired a single bullet into the centre of his forehead. Blood erupted and Muriel's scream cut through me like sharpened steel. A sudden burst of sound echoed around the vast open space, bouncing from the walls and the glass ceiling many yards overhead. It was the sound of hundreds of terrified people all fearful for their lives and the lives of their loved ones. I guessed that less than a quarter of the hostages had actually witnessed the murder, but the noise of the gun was horrendous.

Essa yanked the boy to his feet and pushed him forward. He tripped on his father's corpse and landed in his mother's arms. She was hysterical, clutching the boy and scrambling on her knees towards her dead husband.

'Back,' Hubab Essa hissed. Muriel Steiner ignored her. 'Back, Muriel, or little Mikey will be an orphan.' Essa levelled her pistol at the woman and she stopped moving, just gripped her son so tightly that her fingers turned white as the pair sobbed into each other's shoulders.

CHAPTER 21

'WE *HAVE* TO GET out of here,' I whispered to Chaz as our guard was momentarily distracted by the slaughter off to our right. 'I reckon we have twenty-nine minutes, max.' Chaz nodded as our handler turned his gaze back to us. The skinny runt had a fleck of blood just below his left eye.

We each knew there was only one way out. But even trying that would require some sort of diversion. For some reason, I felt confident that one would come along. The place was a powder keg ready to blow at any moment – a vigilante with a streak of narcissism would do something rash; some nut who'd seen too many *Rambo* movies would try to be a hero. But actually, when it came, the diversion was nothing like that.

Essa stepped closer. She glanced directly at me and I looked away to stare down at the shiny floor. I saw her boots. She paused, then moved on. I looked up and saw her walk away north towards the causeway in front of the entrance to Departures. There were four men there, bomb vests over their chests. They stood like armed police, legs slightly apart, P90s held diagonally across their vests.

Another large group of passengers was bunched up on the floor directly ahead. There must have been fifty of them with two guards watching their every move, parading their guns while the captives kept their heads down. I could see the two men straighten as their leader, Hubab Essa, paced towards them.

She stopped at the back of the group of hostages, studying them with cold, dark eyes. I followed her gaze. She was considering a Middle Eastern couple huddled together, their arms folded, a bag in front of them. She stepped between the seated figures and stopped to stare down at them.

'Stand.'

They stood slowly, eyes averted. The woman was wearing a scarf, the man was heavily bearded. He looked up to meet Essa's eyes. He was putting on a brave face, but I could see he was as frightened as the rest of the hostages.

'Passports.'

The man handed them over.

Essa scanned them. 'Iraqi. What are you doing here?'

'Visiting relatives,' the man said. The woman in the scarf kept her eyes to the floor and let the man do all the talking.

'Where do you live' – Essa glanced at the top passport – 'Yazid? Yazid Hussein. A good Sunni name.'

'We live in a small village close to Tikrit.'

'Tikrit,' Essa repeated. 'That is good. Very good.' She eyed the man, then flicked a look at the woman. 'Ubah. Pretty name. "Flower".' Essa placed two fingers under the woman's chin and lifted her head. The woman forced a brief smile. 'Not much of one, though,' Essa said with a smirk.

A few people were daring to turn slightly to see what was happening. In the silence, Essa's voice carried. It had a shrillness about it. I guessed even she was feeling stressed. 'You may go,' she said.

The man said nothing, just gave the terrorist a grateful look. Ubah peered up voluntarily for the first time, put her hands together and gave Essa a tiny bow.

Essa glanced at one of the men standing guard over the group. 'Escort them.'

Yazid Hussein bent down to lift the single bag the couple had with them. His shirt collar was open. A crucifix on a silver chain tumbled out.

CHAPTER 22

YAZID HUSSEIN TRIED DESPERATELY to grab it, but it was too late. Essa and the guard had seen it. Hussein straightened, the colour draining from his cheeks. His wife looked confused, then realised; terror scurried across her features.

I turned to Chaz. He'd seen everything and knew this was the moment. We had an almost telepathic connection.

'Apostate,' Essa said without expression.

I felt every muscle tense, and a nerve started twitching high up in my right cheek. Essa saw one of her men a dozen yards away and beckoned him over.

'You know the punishment for apostasy?' Essa spat, glaring at the Iraqi couple. 'You know. Of course you know. Your false prophet supposedly died that way.' She turned to the man who had just reached her. 'Parizad. You and Cemal take them.'

Ubah Hussein screeched as Cemal grabbed her arm. And that was when we moved.

Chaz and I sprang forward so fast the guards barely had time to move. Essa was quicker than them. She grabbed a young guy from the floor. He was tall and blond and made a perfect human shield, even if he was yelling in horror and flailing around.

Chaz and I were on the guards in a second. I slammed three fingers into the man called Cemal's carotid artery and he went down like a sack of flour. I grabbed his P90. Chaz had landed a boot in Parizad's throat, crushing his windpipe. We weren't playing games. I spun on our guard. He was stunned but still managed to swing round his gun. I slammed the butt of the P90 I had liberated into his trigger hand, and the bastard squealed and dropped his weapon. Before he could move, I grabbed his gun. Chaz had snatched up a Glock from the terrorist he had just hit, slipping it into his belt as the man writhed on the floor clutching his throat and gasping his final breaths.

From the corner of my eye, I saw the Iraqi, Yazid Hussein. He grabbed his wife's arm and they bolted past me, heading towards the rear of the hall, the southern end and the lift that had brought us down from Level 1. Two men had stood there, but in the confusion they had fanned out left and right, leaving a gap which the couple made for. Yazid and Ubah were young and nimble as whippets. I caught a glimpse of them as they made for the stairs. Essa spotted them too, lifted her P90 in one hand and clutched the blond guy to her with the other. I caught the movement and tugged the trigger of my own assault weapon, spraying bullets half a metre above Essa's head. She fell back, but got to her feet incredibly quickly.

All eyes were on Chaz and me. I retreated, my left arm around our guard's neck, flitting my weapon left and right to encompass the terrorists and the massed crowd of frightened passengers. There were screams and low moans from all around the hall. Chaz came up behind me, a P90 over his shoulder, and suddenly we were racing at breakneck speed to our right and the check-in desks.

We got as far as the Cathay counter before three of the terrorists started firing at us. Our guy was obviously expendable. In one great rush, Chaz and I dived across the baggage-weighing belt, the guard between us. He was yelling, so I landed a swift jaw-rattling punch in the back of his head. He started to fall forward, but Chaz was there to steady him, and we crashed onto the broad conveyor belt. It was still operating. I had the guard pulled close and the three of us rushed along the belt. I could see two men hurtling towards us, their guns poised. They didn't care who they shot. I don't know how he did it, but Chaz had the Glock in his hand. He fired over the terrorists' heads; too dangerous otherwise – we couldn't risk hitting the bombs strapped to their chests. But it was so close the gunmen almost had permanent centre partings. That bought us a crucial couple of seconds and we were at the drop where the bags go down from the belt to the loading bay. Chaz and I braced ourselves, held tight to *our* hostage and we were over the lip and into the void.

CHAPTER 23

Black Detention Centre, North-west London

The SAS had broken Miah Ahmadi at 9.09 a.m., just twenty-one minutes before the attack on Churchill Airport began. Colonel Jack Stewart dashed from the interrogation room, punching in the speed-dial number on his secure mobile. Captain Nigel Grant was a metre behind him.

Stewart's call went through to the Black Detention Centre's Control Room across a ragged quad of weeds and broken playground. From there, Stewart was put straight through to HQ. It took him less than thirty seconds to explain. HQ then immediately declared a Code Red, and contacted MI5, Downing Street, the Commissioner of Police and the Lord Mayor of London. Special Forces were mobilised three minutes later. Downing Street set a meeting of the government's emergency committee, COBRA, in Whitehall starting at 9.25 a.m., five minutes before Essa and her teams swung into action. The Prime Minister was escorted from Number 10 along a broad, over-lit tunnel beneath Downing Street 112 metres to the COBRA building where the meeting was convened.

The first choppers to arrive had been scrambled from RAF Northolt close to the Black Detention Centre and a little under nine miles north-west of Churchill Airport. Jack Stewart and Nigel Grant were in the first wave, landing outside the perimeter. The airport was sealed off; all flights out were cancelled; all incoming flights directed to Gatwick and Stansted. Armoured vehicles started rolling along the Great South West Road to take up position.

The focus of attention was Terminal 4. According to Miah Ahmadi's confession, that was going to be the point of attack. Troops and Special Police Units had the building surrounded by 9.33 a.m. By 9.34 they had learned from a drone and several calls from the public inside the terminal that no terrorist attack had taken place there. At the same time, the commander of the Joint Forces Assault Group close to Terminal 4 was informed that the attack had taken place a mile to the north, in Terminal 3.

The media got to the scene only minutes after the military and police had set up a cordon sixty metres from the building. The normal sounds of Europe's busiest airport – the roar of a plane taking off or landing every forty-five seconds – had been replaced with an eerie quiet broken only by the whir of choppers, the buzz of drones and the noise of seven hundred army and police personnel under the overall command of General Sir Miles Deering.

From their chopper, Colonel Jack Stewart and Captain Nigel Grant, the men who had broken the terrorist prisoner at the eleventh hour, joined the general in his hastily organised Forward Command Post, a workman's portable cabin butted up close to the northern entrance to the car park and immediately south of the main entrance into T3.

General Deering had just opened the lid of his laptop and was about to give Stewart and Grant their orders when they all heard another fresh round of shooting start.

CHAPTER 24

'FUCK!' I EXCLAIMED AS I hit a suitcase on the stationary conveyor in baggage handling. I heard a thud and saw Chaz's sixteen-stone bulk miss everything and slam onto the belt. He was immediately followed by the guard, who landed face first and was out cold. I shoved the guard as I pulled myself off the suitcase and rolled onto the floor, grabbed his combat jacket and yanked him towards me. He tumbled to the ground, groping his way into consciousness, cursing loudly.

We were in a massive basement hanger. The machines had been switched off and stood still. The belts were scattered with cases and bags. There was no one around. The baggage handlers must have made a run for it as soon as the alarms went off.

I pulled up our prisoner and slapped him a couple of times to bring him round. Chaz searched him for weapons and found a knife in the man's boot. I saw a roll of nylon cord close to the conveyor. The luggage guys would have used it for suitcases with broken locks. Using the knife, I cut a length and, while Chaz held him, I tied the terrorist's hands behind his back. I made sure the cord was really tight, tight enough to sting like a bastard. I cut a couple more lengths and tucked them into my pocket – they could be useful.

'Name?' I hissed, spinning the man round to face me.

'Kaber. Nizam Kaber.'

Chaz was checking out the room. 'Ain't sure if they'll come after us or not.'

'They'll come for me,' Kaber said.

'You reckon?' I snapped. 'Personally, I don't think they give a flying fuck about you, sunshine. But they'll want to stop us. That vicious bitch' – I flicked my eyes towards the ceiling – 'certainly isn't dumb. She knows we're dangerous.'

'If we head that way' – Chaz nodded left – 'we'll be directly under Departures. It takes us into the heart of the airport. No telling how much of the terminal is under terrorist control.'

'Move,' I snapped at Kaber, indicating where Chaz had just nodded. We needed to find somewhere quiet and out of sight to start questioning our prisoner.

We took off west, Chaz in front, then our new friend. I had the barrel of my pistol in the small of Kaber's back. We reached a set of double doors that opened onto a broad passage. Chaz clung to the door frame and scanned the corridor with his P90, then waved us forward. We hung a left and then a right, dodging across the bend in combat mode just as we'd done in Baghdad.

I heard them first – boots thumping on concrete. The sound echoed and that made it hard to judge which direction they were coming from. We pulled into a room and bolted the door. It was dark. The door had a reinforced glass window. We heard two men rush past and I caught a glimpse of black combat fatigues – two of Essa's men. Kaber said nothing because he had the barrel of my Glock in his mouth. I found a light switch and fluoros flickered into life. It was a small office.

'The air-con ducts,' Chaz said. 'Last place anyone would search.'

I shoved Kaber into a corner and tied his feet together with lengths of cord from my pocket. Chaz and I dragged over a desk. I climbed up and Chaz tossed me a chair. I could just reach the grille over the duct; I unclasped the latches and turned back to Chaz. He was already scrambling onto the desk. He gave me a leg-up and I was inside the duct. Chaz grabbed Kaber, slung him over his shoulder and I soon had him with me. Chaz gripped my hands and I yanked him up.

We knew how these systems worked – a tangled web of ducts and pipes that spread across the airport like varicose veins. The ducts were no more than just over a metre square, just big enough for us to move in single file, but there would also be plenty of maintenance hubs and concealed units where workers stored equipment.

I cut Kaber's ties and pocketed the cords. Then I led while Chaz came up the back. Kaber knew he would die with a string of P90 bullets up his arse if he tried anything.

Twenty metres along the duct, we came to a junction. I took pot luck and headed left. It was hot and sweaty; the system had shut down. After another eighteen or nineteen metres, the duct opened out onto a maintenance hub and we clambered down into a tiny room three metres square.

'Now,' I said and prodded Kaber with the muzzle of my gun. 'Time to start talking.'

CHAPTER 25

'STRIP TO YOUR UNDERWEAR first,' I said flatly.

'My mother told me about men like you.'

'Yeah, fucking hilarious! Do it.'

As the man removed his combat gear, I passed the items to Chaz. It was the first chance we had to see Kaber up close. I guessed he was in his early twenties. He looked like he'd tried to put some bulk on his frame, but he was congenitally scrawny. He had a shaved head and big, cow-like brown eyes. He didn't strike me as being too bright. He would have been radicalised easily.

Chaz pulled an iPhone from the top-left pocket of Kaber's jacket and a copy of the Quran from the back of the terrorist's black combat pants. He tossed the book into the corner. Kaber reacted as expected, yelling in fury, his face red suddenly as he scrambled to snatch up the book. Chaz shoved him back.

'Does it offend you, scumbag?' Chaz bellowed. 'Yeah, well, you know what offends me? Fucks like you killing innocent people in the name of your crappy religion.'

Kaber hissed and pulled up against the wall. Chaz glanced at the iPhone. 'Could be handy,' he said to me and waved it between us. 'Password,' he demanded, fixing Kaber with a hard look.

The man shrugged. Chaz flew at him, his hand at Kaber's throat. I could see my friend's fingers whiten as he squeezed.

'OK,' the prisoner gasped.

Chaz released the death grip. 'Well?'

'Four, one, three, two.'

Chaz tapped it in. I glanced at my watch. We had twenty-one minutes left.

The phone let out a single shrill note and died.

'You fucker!' Chaz hollered and went for Kaber again.

'Chaz—' I held a hand against my mate's chest. 'Forget it. We need to know about the weapon.'

'Yeah, Chaz,' Kaber snarled. 'You need to know about the—'

I punched the bastard so hard, his nose shattered and blood sprayed out like water from a busted pipe. This time I grabbed his throat. 'Now look, Nizam, you've seen enough Infidel movies to know the cliché. We can do this one of two ways, blah, blah, blah.' I held his eyes with my own hard look, every bit as intimidating as Chaz's.

'Fuck! They're well organised,' I heard Chaz moan, looking at the destroyed phone.

'Where's the weapon?'

Kaber was in agony, but he wasn't going to cave in easily, that much was obvious. The blood had stopped spraying now. It just flowed in a stream over his tightly closed lips and wispy beard to his once-white T-shirt. He said nothing.

'OK. Listen carefully.' I flicked a glance at Chaz, who had pulled the terrorist's own knife from its sheath. The man eyed it. 'This is how it is, Nizam. If that bomb goes off, hundreds, maybe thousands, will die. We' – I flicked my gun at my friend and back to me – 'we can't let that happen. We're ex-military – we know how to reduce big strong men to blubbering heaps begging for their mummies. And we can do it fast. So, tell us where the bomb is.'

Kaber looked straight into my eyes, expressionless.

'I get it,' Chaz said. 'You don't care about dying. I see that. Your seventy-two virgins and all. I know you believe that crap. But we won't just kill you, Kaber.'

The same look.

Chaz leaned forward with the knife. I held the jihadist by the scruff of the neck. Chaz brought Kaber's hand to the floor and, without pausing, sliced off his forefinger. The fucker screamed so loudly I was worried the sound would carry to the last place I wanted it to. I pulled his neck back and punched him in the mouth, knocking teeth into the back of his throat. More blood.

I looked into Kaber's smashed-up face. 'Feel like talking?' I said. 'Where is the weapon?' He spat a tooth at me. I grabbed his neck again. 'Two more fingers, Chaz.'

'*Shwtowp*.'

I kept a grip on Kaber's neck, his head down. Then, after a beat, I pulled him back. 'Where?'

He grinned and I had his face on the concrete in a fraction of a second. He felt the steel on his middle finger and yelled. '*Bwasemwent. In wa bwasemwent*.'

I pulled his head back up again. 'Good. Now, where in the basement?'

He started to shake his head again, and spun to his left and then right so incredibly fast my hand slipped from his wet flesh. His slender build worked for him. He headbutted me and was up on his feet in a single, fluid movement. Chaz was stunned. Kaber kicked him with the flat of his bare foot, sending the huge former soldier and martial-arts champ back into the wall. Then the man was scrambling up to the duct we had crawled along.

Chaz recovered fast, pulled up onto one knee and brought round the P90, but it was too late. Kaber had made it into the duct. Chaz leapt up and started to climb the wall.

I caught the hem of his jacket. 'Leave him, Chaz. We've gotta go.'

CHAPTER 26

WE CAME OUT INTO another empty office. I had kept track of where the ducts had led and figured we were now beyond passport control and security, beyond the main corridor leading off to the gates. I had an image of the map clear in my mind. I knew there was a second airport security office near here.

I opened the door, easing my P90 vertical against my chest. Chaz was on the other side of the door frame, checking the corridor to my left. Then we were out and running, crouched low, sweeping our weapons. The causeway was deserted. It felt odd. I'd never seen an empty departures area anywhere, and certainly not in Churchill. It had always been busy 24/7 since it was built during the 1940s, back in the days when the public areas consisted of tents and duck boarding and it was known as London Airport.

The security office was deserted. Chaz went straight for the comms. I checked my watch: nineteen minutes.

My friend seemed to have a magical ability with machines. It was almost as though he and they shared some strange secret language. He leaned over a control panel, flicked some switches, punched in a few numbers and suddenly radio traffic broke into the room.

'So much cross-talk,' he said. 'I can block us so that Essa won't be able to trace this.' He nodded to the console. 'And we can eavesdrop on them from here.'

'Can you contact the military outside? I'm sure the terminal is surrounded by now. The choppers were airborne fifteen minutes ago.'

Chaz ran his hands over the controls. The sound of a dozen voices began to fade and I could pick out three separate conversations, then one. Two men, one younger than the other; the older man spoke with a cut-glass Home Counties accent. I could visualise his moustache dancing as he spoke. 'Roger that. Out,' he said.

'That one, Chaz,' I said.

He handed me a slick flat-screen device that looked like an iPhone that had been resting on a desk.

'A smart radio,' he said. 'Scrambled . . . I hope.'

'Hello? Who is this?' It was the older man.

'Hi. This is Matt Bates. I'm inside Terminal Three with my friend Chaz Shoeman.'

'What the hell are you doing?

'Trying to help. I'm hoping I've reached your Forward Command Post?'

'I'm afraid that's classified infor—'

'Sir,' I interrupted, deciding to come straight to the point and tell him everything I knew. 'We were in the terminal when the attack happened. Too much to explain now, but we know where the weapon is.'

'What weapon?'

I held my hand over the receiver of the smart radio and rolled my eyes. 'Fuck me! Trust our luck!' Turning back to the mouthpiece, I went on patiently: 'The weapon Hubab Essa told the world about on TV!'

We could hear voices in the background. The soldier was obviously consulting with someone. I decided to just steam on. 'Sir, we are ex-military – SAS Captain Matt Bates, decommissioned 2010, and Charles Shoeman, ex-Delta Force, decommissioned from US Army 2012. Check us out. Who am I speaking to?'

Silence for a moment. Rustling and muffled voices.

'You were discharged without honour, Bates.'

'Right. I wasn't very good at obeying bad orders. However, I am *in here*. Admittedly "without honour", but I can help. Unless you don't want my help . . .' I gave a convincing performance of a man about to hang up.

'Wait! I am General Sir Miles Deering. I am indeed in the Forward Command Post lying to the south of the terminal. What's your status, Bates?'

'The weapon is due to detonate in seventeen and a half minutes, as you know. We are unhurt, well armed and away from the check-in hall. Essa has some four hundred passengers there. We got away. More important, the chemical weapon is in the basement of this building. We can reach it, but have no idea exactly where it is located.'

'I understand.'

Chaz had remained at the bank of controls, leaning over and tapping at a keyboard. There were three monitors above the console.

I guessed they were for the security cameras. Chaz used a toggle and stabbed at keys. Different parts of the airport came up on the screens. In thirty seconds he had found the basement cameras.

'Hang on,' I said into the smart radio.

Chaz's fingers were a blur and he kept skimming the controls even when he looked up to the monitors every few seconds.

'There!' I yelled, and heard the general shout an expletive down the line. 'Sorry, General,' I mumbled as I watched the monitor. 'My buddy has found the location of the weapon.'

On the screen, we could see five heavily armed men in combat fatigues. Two of them were standing to one side next to a pillar. Attached to it was a box. At its centre was a green tube. Wires descended from the base of the box. It just had to be the weapon. Close by, on the floor, lay Radi's opened briefcase. And to the far right of the screen we could just about see a man in a suit. Dirar Radi himself.

CHAPTER 27

'SO,' SAID GENERAL DEERING. 'Do you chaps have a plan?'

I looked at Chaz. Up to now we'd had no time to think of anything other than our own survival, but my mind was working, the cogs whirring fast.

'One moment, sir.' I turned to Chaz. 'Can you get a full schematic of the airport on any of these machines?'

'I'll try.'

'General Deering. Chaz is searching for a full schematic of the airport.'

'My technician here wonders if Mr Shoemaker could' – there was a pause as the general consulted with someone – 'use... FaceTime. Or... or some other method to transmit the security-camera footage to us?'

Chaz nudged me and I turned to see a 3D image on the main monitor. He then tapped a few keys and I assumed he was somehow communicating the security footage to the tech guys at the Forward Command Post. 'OK,' I said down the line. 'We have a 3D schematic of the airport.'

I studied the screen. We were up on Level 1; the jihadists were a floor below us on Ground. I traced the lines on the screen with a finger. The basement camera had shown the bomb to be inside the main boiler room on B3, the lowest level. I moved my finger up and saw a loading dock on B2. 'Chaz. An entry point,' I said. 'What do you think?' He nodded and I turned back to the smart radio.

'Sir?'

'Bates, we have the schematic now on our screens. And my tech says thanks for the security-camera footage.'

'Good. Right. The bomb is on B3, main boiler room. We need a rear assault with a diversion up top. If you look at the back of the terminal, there's a road ramp that leads down to a loading bay on B2. That could be an access point for a small team.'

'Got it.'

'But as a backup, we need more than a couple of guns between Chaz and me.'

As I was talking, Chaz was poking around. He'd opened a metal cabinet. Inside was an array of guns.

'We've found some weaponry here in the security office.'

'Excellent.'

'But if, for some reason, your men don't break through to B3 and it ends up with us going in alone, I don't like the odds – three to one. I have an idea about that, though.'

'What?'

'Leave that to us, sir. We need to meet up with your men.' I checked my watch again and we synced up with the Command Post. It was precisely thirty seconds past ten o'clock. 'Sixteen and a half minutes remaining. Assuming the men down on B3 work to schedule.'

'Righto, Bates. I've coordinated with my second, Colonel Jack Stewart. He's one of yours.'

I smiled at Chaz. He meant SAS. I felt good about that.

'He'll take a small group around the western flank of the terminal and link up with you at precisely ten thirteen. We'll create a diversion close to the south entrance to the terminal. You then have approximately four minutes to get down to B3, eliminate the defenders and neutralise the bomb. Our tech team is working on the security-camera footage you found. Anything they get on the nature of the weapon we'll shoot over to you on the smart radio.'

'Got it.'

'Anything to add?'

'No, sir.'

Chaz leaned in and spoke to the general for the first time. 'Sir, I suggest we maintain radio silence except in case of emergency. I can't be one hundred per cent sure how secure the comms are, or how long the scrambling will hold. The terrorists are very well organised and using some clever tech.'

'Understood. Good luck, the pair of you.'

CHAPTER 28

WE WERE BACK OUT on the concourse. We had each added Colt M16s and backup handguns, a pair of SIGs, to our firepower, our pockets stuffed with ammo. I'd found a nice heavy commando knife, a Fairbairn Sykes. As we ran, I explained to Chaz what I was planning. He grinned. 'Clever.'

'All we need is a proper kitchen. Trouble is,' I said quietly, 'every time I come here, the layout has changed slightly.'

Chaz spotted a Starbucks. 'Nah,' I said. 'Unlikely. Isn't there some pseudo-French place along here somewhere?'

'I think so. There's a Yo! Sushi over there. What about that?'

I shook my head. 'The French place is called Pierre's or Le Palais or something.'

We ran, crouching, past Gucci and Hermès, swung a left and then a right and saw EAT, and then an O'Neill's Irish Pub.

'The pub,' I said. 'That might work.'

I led the way, scoping the empty tables and bar with my P90. Chaz backed in close behind me, checking that the causeway was clear and no one had seen us duck inside the pub.

The place was usually buzzing, but now it was like some deserted Wild West saloon after the gunslinger had come through the swing doors. The TV was on, a huge flat-screen perfect for showing football. Today, though, the terror attack on Churchill Airport had blanket coverage, red and blue flashing lights and an overexcited news reporter with Terminal 3 as her backdrop. The volume was up and as we ran I heard her latest update: 'At least four hundred civilians are thought to be held hostage in the main check-in hall. Many others escaped earlier, especially those passengers in Departures who were preparing to board. It's believed up to five thousand people, including hundreds of airport staff, have fled the building. They are currently being processed in a hangar some half a mile to my right.' She pointed towards Terminal 5.

We dashed down a narrow passage beside the bar, through a pair of doors with a round window in each and emerged into a storeroom stacked high with boxes. The words on them flashed through my mind as we rushed across the room: Cadbury, Walkers. Then we were in a cooler room with crates almost to the ceiling. We saw beer bottles and boxes of spirits, cases of soft drinks and mixers. In one corner stood a wheelie bin, clear cellophane dangled over its lip. A second later we were in a mid-sized kitchen, all stainless-steel surfaces and sharp knives. Food lay in dishes, there was flour on the floor and a bottle on its side; extra-virgin olive oil had collected in a wide puddle beside the steel counter. The staff had definitely left in a hurry.

'OK, Chaz, can you find half a dozen small bottles of water? About this size?' I held my hands about fifteen centimetres apart. He got straight onto it, pulling open fridge doors and overhead cupboards.

I turned to the other side of the kitchen. 'Food? Ingredients? Where the fuck do they keep that stuff?'

I yanked open door after door. Pots and pans, glasses, lots of glasses. I whirled round and tried a different set of units to my right, and with the fifth set of doors, I struck gold. Boxes of chocolate powder, mustard, tea, instant coffee. 'Vinegar. Great.' I pulled the four-litre bottle from the cupboard and tossed it onto a counter beside me. 'Now, baking powder.'

I dragged the cartons, bottles and boxes from the cupboard. Nothing. 'Shit!' I exclaimed, and moved on to the next cupboard to my right. Rows of bottled lemon juice, ketchup, Worcestershire sauce. 'Damn!'

Next cupboard. Boxes. I rifled through them, tossing them to the floor behind me and reached deep into the cupboard to drag more from the back. I could sense I was close. Then, right at the back, behind an industrial-sized tub of Nutella, stood three boxes of baking powder. I grabbed two, pulled them out and spun to the counter as Chaz rushed over with an armful of bottles nestled up against his chest. We dumped everything on the counter.

'Right, Chaz,' I said. 'Empty the bottles.' I uncapped the vinegar and ripped open the baking soda. 'Shit! I forgot paper napkins.'

'I saw those,' Chaz said, and he rushed away to a cupboard close to one of the fridges. I started to pour vinegar into the empty water bottles, until each was about a quarter full. Chaz was back with a pile of napkins. That's when we both heard the sound simultaneously – something small and hard, a phone maybe, clunking across the concrete floor.

CHAPTER 29

WE SPUN ROUND IN a heartbeat, our P90s trained on the same spot, a narrow opening between a cupboard and the back wall of the kitchen.

'Come out with your hands up,' Chaz commanded.

We heard a weird sound. Was it a woman crying?

A young woman emerged first, then a middle-aged guy with horn-rimmed glasses, a chef's apron over his jeans and buttoned-down shirt. Last came a heavily pregnant woman in a floral dress, a knapsack on her back, her hair tied back. Tears streamed down her cheeks.

'Please. Don't hurt us,' the girl said.

Chaz and I lowered our guns.

'What are you doing here?' It came out rougher than I meant it to and the three of them visibly backed off. I repeated myself, softer.

The pregnant woman stepped forward. 'Linda. Linda Frith.' She extended a hand, the other tucked under her belly. 'The alarms went off. I was . . . we, my sister, Jess' – she nodded towards the younger woman – 'we were too scared to go.'

'I stayed with them,' the man said. 'Then it was all too late. I'm Jerry.'

I ignored his hand. 'We're racing against the clock,' I said and turned back to the counter.

As speedily as I could, I poured baking powder in lines along six paper napkins. Chaz and I started rolling them. Flipped them over and folded again.

Jess had approached. 'What you doing?'

'Making flash bombs. You've seen the TV, yeah?'

She shook her head. 'No.'

'There's a chemical weapon in the basement. The check-in hall has been taken over – hundreds held there.'

The girl looked pale.

'And you?' Jerry asked.

'We happened to be in the right place at the right time,' Chaz said.

'Well, that depends on your perspective,' I added as I stuffed the first of the filled napkins into a bottle of vinegar. Chaz was working as fast as me and we started to screw the tops really tight.

'May I use your knapsack?' I asked Linda.

She looked surprised, then pulled it off. ''Course.'

She took out her purse, her passport and a small make-up pouch. Ditching the make-up, she slipped the purse and passport into a pocket at the front of her floral dress.

'Thanks,' I said and loaded it up with the six bottles. 'We have to go.'

'Take us. Please.'

I shook my head. 'We're entering the most dangerous part of the terminal. You're far better off staying here.'

'Not if the bomb goes off,' Jerry said and held my gaze.

'Got a point, buddy,' Chaz said, turning to me.

I sighed. 'I guess so.'

CHAPTER 30

I GLANCED AT MY watch. It was approaching 10.08. Five minutes to get to the rendezvous point. Nine minutes to stop a catastrophe.

We moved as fast as we could with the three from the pub, but naturally the pregnant woman, Linda, was a liability.

'I'm really sorry,' she said. 'Maybe you should go on.'

'We're committed now,' I said.

I led the group. Chaz came up the rear. Jerry and the two women ran, huddled together. In that way, we headed north along the left flank.

The smart radio buzzed. I glimpsed at the screen as we ran. 'Info about the bomb from the Command Post,' I said to Chaz and tossed him the device.

We stopped for a few seconds while he studied the screen. 'The analysts are pretty sure it's a Soman bomb with an electronic timer,' he said, and handed back the radio.

We passed deserted shops and eating places until we reached the main duty-free area, a retail space as big as all the other shops and cafés put together.

Straight ahead was a bank of lifts. *Can't risk those,* I thought and veered right, dodging a trolley piled high with boxes. Our three new friends pushed on. Linda and Jerry went around the stacked trolley, left and right, but Jess was distracted and didn't see it. She smacked into the thing with a loud thump and was thrown backwards. Chaz was with her in a second.

He crouched down. 'You OK?'

Jess was dazed and holding her wrist, her face contorted in agony. 'Shit! she exclaimed. 'I think I've . . .'

Chaz took her wrist and probed gently. We had all stopped. I stood guard, sensitive to the slightest movement. I felt for the girl, but my guts were churning. The seconds were ticking down.

'You've dislocated it,' Chaz said.

'I'm OK,' Jess groaned and started to get up. Chaz helped her. It was only then we all saw the nasty laceration across her left thigh; her jeans were ripped open, blood was flowing down her leg.

Chaz and I spotted a sharp metal edge protruding from a crate on the cart. Jess put weight on her leg. 'I'll be all right,' she mumbled. She didn't sound too convincing. 'We have to . . .' She took a unsteady step forward. I caught Chaz's eye and we moved forward to a doorway leading onto a service staircase. The door had a square window at head height. It slammed behind us and we stood in a white-walled stairwell. To our right, a flight of stairs ascended to an admin level, another set to our left led down. I could see lights down there, but they blanked out after Ground. I knew from the schematic that this staircase only went down to B1.

'This is where it starts to get tricky,' I said. 'One floor down is the check-in hall. There are twenty or thirty heavily armed jihadists there with the hostages. We have to get past that ground-floor level.' I paused and we all heard sounds from below. Someone had opened the door leading onto the stairwell. We heard the door on Ground swing shut and the sound dampen again, then footsteps approaching. Someone was climbing the stairs.

'Up,' I hissed.

Chaz retreated to the door on our level, and slipped behind it as I stepped up the first flight of stairs with the others. I could see down and through the window in the door where Chaz stood to the right.

A man was taking the stairs cautiously. He had a Kalashnikov at the ready and was looking around him. I saw him approach the landing, and by moving my head an inch to the right, I could also see Chaz through the window in the door. The man took two steps, then a third. I nodded to Chaz.

His timing was perfect. He smashed the door inwards with brutal force and the leading edge hit the terrorist like a truck. He fell back against the railing and Chaz was inside before the man had stopped moving. I saw a flash of metal and Chaz's knife slide left to right, cutting through the man's neck. He folded, like spaghetti from a fork. I heard Linda gasp behind me.

'Right. Let's go,' I said quietly.

CHAPTER 31

JERRY, LINDA AND JESS averted their eyes as they passed the dead man and stopped at the top of the stairs taking us down straight into the lion's den. Jess leaned back against the wall. She was clearly in agony.

I stepped over the corpse and took the lead again, stopping at the foot of the first flight of stairs. I crouched and could see what was going on through the square window of the door at the bottom of the steps, catching glimpses of the check-in area – jihadists in black, and in the middle distance several large groups of terrified civilians. It looked very much as it had when we were there. I could hardly believe that was only twenty-five minutes ago.

'We go as fast as we can, but as carefully as we can,' I whispered close to the three from the pub. Linda looked petrified, her hands shaking. Jerry swallowed hard and Jess just gave Chaz and me an agonised nod. The leg of her jeans was soaked with blood.

I stepped down, my finger on the trigger of the P90. The last thing I wanted was to be caught, but if we were spotted, I knew I would take out as many of the terrorists as I could and Essa would be my prime target.

I'd been in tense situations before and so had Chaz; but never anything where the stakes were quite so high. I felt the nerves in the pit of my stomach and gripped the gun, a layer of sweat between my fingers and the metal.

At the foot of the stairs, I crouched low. The others copied me; Linda on her hands and knees. It felt as though time had slowed. It took us ten seconds to get past the doorway and onto the next flight of stairs down, but it felt like ten minutes, easy.

We gathered on the first landing down from Ground and then pressed on faster, breathing almost normally again.

CHAPTER 32

I SWUNG THE DOOR outwards onto a narrow corridor, a rough brick wall straight ahead, a pallid strip light in the ceiling. We were on B1, a service floor filled with maintenance rooms, storage areas and loading bays where the supplies for the terminals arrived throughout the day and night. I hung a right and glanced back. Chaz was a yard behind the group of three. Jess swayed and closed her eyes. I stopped and caught her as she started to fall.

Chaz dashed up to us. 'Looks like she's lost a lot of blood,' he said, inspecting the damage to the girl's leg.

Linda stumbled forward. 'Jess . . .'

Chaz turned to her. 'She's hurt bad.'

Linda crouched on all fours again and ran a hand through her sister's hair.

I checked my watch. Ninety seconds to the rendezvous. The SAS team would be on its way. I snatched up the smart radio and switched it on. A burst of static and some muffled sounds came from the other end. Chaz took it from my hands and fiddled with two small controls on the front.

'Bates?' It was General Deering. Chaz handed the radio back to me. 'Our men have left,' the general said. 'What's your status?'

'We've found three civilians, including a very pregnant woman.' I glanced at Linda. She looked up. I could see in the dull light that she was sweating profusely, her face pale. 'We also have an injured woman who's lost a lot of blood. She needs urgent medical attention.'

'Consider it done.' I heard more muffled sounds. 'Are you in position?'

'We're close.' I heard a double click down the line. 'Sir, was that you?'

The line was dead.

'Shit!' I hissed.

'What?' Chaz said. I could hear the anxiety in his voice.

'Lost connection.'

'Let's go.'

Chaz bent down and lifted Jess into his arms. She was barely aware of what was going on, her eyes rolling. 'Medics are on their way,' Chaz said softly, but I don't think the girl heard him.

'This way.' I took the lead again.

We reached the end of the corridor. It branched left and right. I knew the way, the schematic etched indelibly into my mind. I swung left. Jerry was immediately behind me, panting heavily. Then came Linda, half-stumbling, and Chaz carrying the girl. I was worried about a lot of things: what we would do once we reached the rendezvous, the loss of our comms, and how the hell we were supposed to disarm the bomb in time. It also unnerved me that Chaz was carrying Jess, our flank exposed. But I could do nothing about any of it.

'Come on,' I said and turned round as I ran. 'Not far now.'

There was a tight corner ahead, a left turn, and then, five metres on, the floor gave way to a steel mesh bridge, a mezzanine some twenty metres long. We stopped and I eased forward. Seven or eight metres below us stretched B2, an open expanse that looked like a lightly stocked warehouse. Fifteen metres in a straight line from the mezzanine lay the ramp down from Ground. I could hear nothing coming from there but knew the SAS team would be creeping down almost silently. They would be visible any moment. I checked the time. Almost 10.13. Ten seconds to rendezvous.

CHAPTER 33

I SAW THE LEADER of the five-man team at the edge of a puddle of dull light and felt a surge of relief. But it lasted only a second – gunfire screamed out from directly beneath us. I saw one of the SAS group shudder as he was strafed by bullets. Two of the other four hit the ground to return fire; two of the remaining four covered their flank.

'Back!' I screamed. 'They've been ambushed.'

Chaz lowered Jess gently to the floor. Linda and Jerry didn't need a second warning; they pulled back into the corridor.

An explosion ripped across B2 as a grenade landed at the feet of the British soldiers. I saw one of them blown apart, but the two on the floor were fast enough to pull up and dive to the side. I shoved myself back against the wall, one foot on the steel mesh bridge. Chaz took up position across from me.

'They must have broken through the scrambler – heard me talking to Deering. Fuck!' I hissed.

Chaz peered over the edge of the railings that ran each side of the mezzanine. Four men in black fatigues and balaclavas rushed under the metal bridge, machine guns blazing. The SAS guys returned fire. One of the attackers fell. The other three pressed on, sprinting and firing.

I signalled to Chaz and we rushed forwards across the bridge, P90s on the rails, torrents of shells slamming into the three remaining jihadists. Now it was us who had the element of surprise on our side.

'Wait here. Just a minute,' I yelled back to the three in the corridor. 'Keep down.'

Chaz led the way down the metal steps. I surveyed the route the gunmen had taken from deep inside B2, directly under the main halls of Terminal 3. There were no more of them. We reached the floor of the basement. I ran on to the soldiers, while Chaz checked the terrorists. Two of the SAS men were pretty smashed up. The other three were dead.

I crouched beside one of the injured men and saw the name on his jacket: STEWART. 'Medics on their way,' I said.

Chaz ran over. I looked up at him. 'Fuckers are dead,' he said.

I glanced at the time. 10.14. We had three minutes.

A noise from up ahead. Chaz swept the ramp with his P90. I was down on one knee and brought my gun round. Then we saw the red crosses on the helmets and lowered our weapons.

Four medics, each armed to the teeth, dashed forward.

'Bloody good to see you guys,' I said.

'Your buddies were ambushed,' Chaz added, spitting out the words. 'Didn't stand a chance. But we were on the bridge.' He pointed back the way we had come. 'Gave 'em a dose. Bastards are all dead.'

I stood and paced over to one of the medics, a major, the group's commander. 'Matt Bates,' I said.

'Major Brennan.'

'Listen, Major, I've gotta go.' I looked at my watch again involuntarily. 'Three of these guys are dead. Two badly injured. We have three civilians with us. Up there.' I pointed to the mezzanine gantry. 'Two women and a man. One of the women has lost a lot of blood, a nasty laceration to her thigh. The other woman is more than eight months pregnant.'

He nodded, shouted instructions to the other three, and ran for the metal steps up to the bridge.

I hitched the knapsack that held the flash bombs. 'Ready?' I asked Chaz.

'Line 'em up,' he replied.

CHAPTER 34

IT WAS HOT. I only really noticed it as we started running along the corridors in B2; obviously heat from the boiler room seeping up. Now that our cover was blown and Essa would know we were down here, we might have to contend with more terrorists following those sent down earlier. I voiced my fears to Chaz as we slunk along the winding passages.

'Not so sure about that, Matt,' he said. 'Remember, Deering was gonna cause a distraction. Also, Essa's men must be pretty overstretched by now. Her biggest headache will be keeping the hostages together and fighting off the inevitable assault on the building.'

'Hope you're right,' I said.

We saw no one. B2 was another storage area. Big stuff – heavy machinery, spare conveyors, generators, large office equipment. I clocked a room filled with cabinets, shelves stacked with boxes. I took little notice; they just flashed past. Checking my watch had now become a compulsion – understandable, really: one minute fifty seconds.

'Come on, Chaz, gotta move faster.'

'Where's the nearest way down?'

We turned onto a broad causeway, large rooms off to our left. 'Up ahead, to the right. A staircase.'

We reached the door opening onto a stairwell. I scanned the space beyond through a small window. Nothing. Chaz kicked the door and it slammed against the wall. I ran in swinging my P90, Chaz half a second behind me. He leaned over the railing, peering down to the lowest level, B3. He pulled back: 'Clear.'

I sped down the stairs. Chaz came up behind, then he ran ahead to the foot of the last flight. The stairwell on B3 was empty.

I stopped for a second and unlatched Linda's knapsack, took out three of the water bottles and handed them to Chaz. He stuffed them into his belt. I followed suit and tossed the bag. Easing the door outwards, I covered the corridor with my assault rifle. Empty. I swung right. Chaz pulled over to the other side of the corridor and we crept on.

The noise was a surprise, a pounding from the boilers you could feel in your chest, in your guts. The air seemed to crackle with energy and there was a strong smell – oil, ozone.

We pulled up at a point where the corridor veered hard left and I risked a peep around the corner. There was a dead man slumped against the left wall, his chest blown open. The boiler room lay straight ahead. Two men stood at the midpoint between us and it. I nodded to Chaz and we rushed out, cutting down the two men. Reaching the door to the boiler room, we held back. It was so noisy there was every chance no one inside would have heard the gunfire, but we weren't betting on it.

We sneaked inside, the sound pounding around us. The stink seemed to seep into my skin. Chaz moved behind a large oil tank. He knew as well as me that we had to be precise with our weapons. A few shells in a boiler or a tank of oil would be a disaster. We also had to make sure the jihadists had no time to fire back. They might not be so careful.

Two more men in fatigues stood with Radi. One of them had his back to us and stood close to the box attached to the pillar we'd seen on the security cam. Radi said something to the guy which was drowned out by the noise.

I removed a flash bomb and saw Chaz do the same. I shook mine vigorously and felt the pressure inside it increase. The blend of vinegar and baking soda began to harden under the plastic as carbon dioxide built up inside the bottle. I tightened the top and saw Chaz copy me. Then I pulled out the remaining two bottles in my belt and started to shake them. Timing was everything.

Lifting the first bottle, I held up three fingers and pulled them down – three, two, one . . . and I tossed the bottle in a low arc towards the group around the bomb. Chaz's followed mine. They landed with a heavy smack and exploded. A chemical mixture of salt and gas burst from the neck of each bottle, and with it, a burst of light and a bang that pierced its way over the thud of the boilers. I grabbed my other two bottles and watched as Chaz's almost collided with them in mid-air. All four landed together on the concrete at the feet of the terrorists. One failed to go off, but the other three didn't disappoint. They boomed and sprayed blazing chemicals everywhere.

We didn't give the men a second to react, just charged out from our hiding places, each of us pulling back on triggers. Chaz had switched to his M16. He shot the jihadist nearest the box in the kneecaps. The man collapsed forward and I landed a stream of P90 shells along his back. Chaz took out the other guy with a precise burst between the eyes. I swung to shoot Radi, but he had been furthest from the flash bombs and had reacted with impressive reflexes, spinning to his left and ducking behind a boiler.

We dashed across the five metres to the bomb. I caught a glimpse of the timer: thirty-two seconds.

CHAPTER 35

CHAZ WAS THE EXPERT and he grabbed the sides of the box to peer inside. Then came the *phat, phat, phat* of shells slamming into concrete. It cut over the horrendous noise. I swung right and saw Radi. Lifting my P90, I squeezed the trigger. Nothing happened.

I had to make a snap decision – go for the Colt, or rush the fucker? There was really only one choice. I flew at the man, vaguely aware of Chaz swearing and tapping keys on a control pad. I knew I was quite literally leaping into the void, and a large part of me expected a very quick death. *Any moment*, I was thinking. *Any moment I'll be cut down by Kalashnikov shells at close range.*

But that moment didn't come. I was fifteen centimetres away from Radi, his body odour filling my lungs and obliterating the stench of oil and fumes. I grabbed his gun, twisted the barrel and snapped his finger on the trigger. He screamed in my ear and I felt the gun vibrate as he let off a stream of shells.

I knew Chaz was safe because I had pushed Radi off balance and he'd swung to his left, but I was worried about the boilers. I yanked up the weapon, its muzzle pointed towards the low ceiling, and gained control of it.

With my arms raised, Radi drew a knife and slashed it across my abdomen. I felt a sharp pain that shot through me like lightning in a bottle. But I was raging now, pumped and bursting with killer energy. I slammed the butt of the gun into Radi's face – once, twice. He staggered back and I had my commando knife out. I half-tripped, half-jumped onto him, yelling at the top of my voice, pain throbbing through me and down each leg. My knife hand flew out and I saw the blade sink into Radi's left eye. It just kept going up to the hilt, and I felt his body slither out from under me. Pulling up, I realised I was still yelling.

'Matt! That lever!' Chaz was screaming at me. 'Get it! Pull it up!'

For a second, I felt as though I was going to pass out. The room seemed to revolve. Lights cascaded across my vision, over the boilers, the tanks, Chaz, the bomb. They swam around and bristled sparkling light. I was a kid again and Dad had just lit a Roman candle. I gazed on in wonder at the rising sparks and smoke.

'Matt!'

I staggered forward. At the edge of my vision I could just see the counter. It said '4'. I lifted my hand. I was swimming through mercury. I felt the metal of the lever under my fingertips, moved my hand around it and pulled up. I saw a '3'. The lever slotted into place. The clock flicked over to '2'. Then . . .

CHAPTER 36

IT STOPPED.

'Holy fucking Christ!' Chaz gasped and turned to me wearing a big grin. Then his eyes looked down at my front and his face dropped. I fell to my knees and Chaz caught me, squeezing my blood-soaked shirt between us.

'It's all right,' I managed to gasp.

'Yeah, sure, buddy. It's all fine and dandy.'

'We did it, Chaz. We fuckin' did it.'

I saw his grin return as he hauled me up.

The sound of heavy boots on concrete broke over the thudding in the boiler room. We looked up together and saw six British soldiers, assault weapons swinging left and right before them as they charged into the room; and for one horrible moment, I thought they might mistake us for Islamic extremists. But the front runner lowered his gun as he stopped thirty centimetres in front of us.

'Here, let me help,' he said and supported my left shoulder as Chaz took the right. I saw his men fan out and make sure the jihadists were dead. I was pretty sure that would check out.

As we reached the corridor, a team of medics arrived. I was handed over. Chaz ran alongside the men as they carried me away, and the guy who had helped drag me from the boiler room spun round and dashed back the way we'd come.

As we emerged onto the loading area on B2, it was sheer pandemonium. Noises came from every direction; there was an explosion and heavy gunfire.

'Fuck! They've stormed the building,' I groaned as I was laid on a stretcher and lifted by two medics. Chaz was leaning over me.

'What did you expect, buddy?'

Another explosion, nearer this time, louder. The sound of shattering glass. I had an oxygen mask placed over my mouth and looked up to see the lights of the ceiling stream past. Chaz was panting, his face smeared with grease, the whites of his eyes exaggerated by the mess. I felt his hand on my arm and then it was shoved away roughly as one of the medics got a line into me as she ran.

I'd been somewhere similar before, but knew instinctively that this was nothing in comparison. Chaz had been there then too. He had dragged me from the armoured car near Basra. All my men had died in that vehicle and I had never really got over the survivor's guilt. My behaviour after that had reflected my inner pain and guilt. Never far from my mind was the thought: *I should have died with them*. I'd been back on active duty a year later, but I was no longer the pliant career soldier who had been fast-tracked since university.

We were out in the air and I could smell sulphur, the stench of explosives. We ran through a great cloud of smoke. Shouts.

Another, smaller explosion further away; I guessed it had come from the far side of the terminal. *Hopefully that bitch Hubab Essa has chewed on a few bullets*, I thought.

CHAPTER 37

HUBAB ESSA WAS APPROACHING the endgame, and she knew it. Knew it and didn't care. She would soon be in paradise. Ilham would be there and they would be together for all eternity. She didn't like to think too much about his seventy-two virgins.

The hundreds of hostages were still at her mercy. She watched their terrified, pathetic faces and felt nothing but contempt. She was sick of the stink of them. They all deserved to die; all the Infidels deserved to die and the Caliphate would rule supreme as foretold, as Allah had intended it to be.

And that's when it began. A blast from the south, a boom and the sound of tonnes of glass crashing to the terminal floor followed by screams and yells from the mass of petrified human beings gathered together in the check-in hall.

Another boom. A flash of light. A smoke grenade landed at the far side of the hall and started to plume. Then a flash bomb went off and Essa turned away. Clutching at her radio, she clicked it to 'on', threw a switch and feedback screeched from the airport's PA.

'*Allahu Akbar!*' she bellowed into the radio and the two dread words resonated around the huge public area above the screams and the cries, the shells splattering into walls and flash grenades slamming to the floor.

At the exits, the suicide bombers heard the words and said their final prayers. A second later, six explosions rang out almost simultaneously as the men pushed thumbs down onto red buttons and their vests exploded.

Hubab Essa started to run and grabbed a girl who was crouching behind a pillar. She was about sixteen, tall and skinny with a blonde bob. Essa pulled her close, brought her left hand round the front of the girl's neck and pulled the edge of her knife up so hard it cut into the kid's skin, allowing a line of blood to trickle down her throat. The girl screamed.

'Shut up!' Essa barked. 'Another sound and I'll slice you open.'

Essa backed away with the girl lifted a foot off the ground. She had her P90 in her right hand and was covering the space in front of her with its short muzzle. Across the floor of the hall, she could see a line of men wearing body armour and gas masks rushing towards her. One of her men, her number two, Zahoor Ashmina – who had disposed of her dangerously nervous cousin, Nadir Abdallah, back in Ealing – dived behind a check-in desk and opened fire on the advancing firearms team, winging one of them. Their return fire was brutal; the check-in desk seemed to disintegrate under a barrage of shells and Essa watched as Ashmina was ripped apart.

Essa and her prisoner reached a flight of stairs off to the west side of the check-in hall. It led up to an office overlooking the open space. She ducked and pulled the girl down with her as a stream of shells came too close for comfort. A second, much louder boom echoed around the hall and Essa felt the stairs vibrate. She reached the top and looked out at the crowd of panicking people. Hundreds of men, women and children ran this way and that. Armed police and British troops were swarming into the hall. She saw another of her men taken out and felt for the red button on its short cable, reached the plastic nub and traced it with her thumb. Essa let go of the girl. She scrambled away along a strip of carpet, grasping at the door to the office. Essa started to mount the metal banisters. She was directly above a group of people, mothers clasping young children, men shielding their wives. She was almost there.

What a surprise they will get, Essa considered. It was her last thought. A fraction of a second later, a bullet from a British Army sniper positioned high up on a crossbeam in the roof, fifty metres to the south, entered the woman's head at the coronal suture, separating the frontal bone from the parietal. Essa had no time to squeeze the button of her bomb vest, nor time to move a muscle before the Radically Invasive Projectile, or RIP, separated into its nine component parts, turning her brain to mush.

CHAPTER 38

AS I WAS BEING patched up, I felt a bit of a wuss. Radi's knife hadn't so much as nicked a major blood vessel, and it had missed every organ only to tear a twenty-centimetre rip across my abdomen. What was all the fuss about?

Chaz sat beside me in the ambulance where it had parked on the airport periphery. The noise from the terminal had diminished; the last explosion had gone off several minutes ago. There had been no gunfire for maybe ninety seconds. We were watching events unfold live on TV using an iPad someone had handed us. I'd lost a fair bit of blood. A bag of AB negative hung on a stand close to my head. My wounds had been bandaged and the morphine was beginning to kick in.

'Pretty slick operation,' Chaz commented, looking towards the ravaged terminal building.

'What did you expect, Captain America? Muskets and buck-shot?'

Chaz laughed and he made me laugh too. I immediately regret-ted it. 'Bugger me sideways with a fish fork!' I gasped, panting and clutching my guts. 'Note to self – never laugh again . . . ever.'

I pulled myself up a little and winced.

'Take it easy, buddy,' Chaz said. 'You ain't superman any more. Maybe ten years ago.'

'Fuck off!' I exclaimed and grinned. 'You were starting to get a bit puffed back there.'

'Yeah, right.'

Listen,' I said, suddenly serious. 'Could you ask that very pretty medic who bandaged me up if I could borrow her mobile?'

He got up and exited the back of the ambulance. A few moments later, the female army doctor popped her head around the door. 'What do you want with my phone, Captain Bates? Or is it *Mr* Bates?'

'Don't be unkind,' I said and flicked my eyes down to the well-padded bandage about my abdomen.

She smiled and handed it over.

'Thanks,' I said. 'Won't be long.'

'Good!'

I punched in the numbers. It rang three times, then four, five. I was just about to give up with a sigh of disappointment when the line opened and I heard a kid's voice.

'Hey, Tommy, my man,' I said.

'Dad!'

'Hi, son. You OK?'

'Yeah. You seen the TV? The attack on the airport?'

'I'm watching it right now on an iPad.'

'An iPad? You don't have one. Didn't know you'd even heard of them.'

'Cheeky beggar!'

Tommy laughed and I almost joined him before remembering.

'Hey, Dad, weren't you going to Churchill Airport today?'

'I was, but your Uncle Chaz called last night. He can't make it for a few weeks, so we've postponed the trip. Lucky, actually. Our flight was at eleven. Could have got caught up in it.'

'Looks pretty nasty.'

'Yep. Well, look, I just wanted to see if you were all right.'

'Of course I am, Dad. You sound odd. Are *you* all right?'

'Couldn't be better. We still on for two weeks' time?' I knew Chaz and I would not be leaving for Mykonos any time soon, and we would have to reschedule.

'I have it on my laptop appointments page.'

'Oh, do you now, Tom? Don't you go getting all executive on me.'

The boy laughed and I felt my stomach cramp as I joined in.

'OK, Tommy, gotta go. Love you.'

'Love you, Dad. And I'm so glad Uncle Chaz had to postpone.'

CHAPTER 39

Six weeks later, Mykonos

Chaz and I were sitting in our favourite beach bar, Giorgio's. The sun was beginning its daily slide into the crystal, turquoise water, a giant crimson orb perched on the horizon. It was happy hour at Giorgio's, three euros a beer – who could complain about that?

We were at a white plastic table close to the sand, our third round of beers ordered and on their way. Just three days into the fortnight in Greece and the layers of problems, stresses and strains were falling away like peeled onion. There were only two others in Giorgio's, a pair of very attractive women sipping cocktails.

In the corner, close to the bar, there was an old TV. A magazine show had just started and we could see words at the foot of the screen: 'Airport Attack: six weeks on.'

Giorgio arrived with our drinks and saw us studying the screen.

'Quite a thing, that attack,' he said gravely. His English was almost perfect. He'd told us on our first night that he had once owned a Greek restaurant in Hampstead.

'Sure was,' Chaz said.

'They're saying there were two guys inside the terminal, ex-military. Saved a lot of people. Can you believe that? May have even stopped the chemical bomb going off!'

'Really?' I said.

'I don't get it, though,' Giorgio added. 'If I'd done that, I wouldn't . . . what's the expression? Hide my rays under a bush.'

'Light under a bushel,' Chaz said.

'Yeah, that,' Giorgio replied, pointing at Chaz.

'Well, maybe they didn't want the attention. You know, all those women throwing themselves at 'em.'

Giorgio looked at me seriously for a moment, then broke into a deep belly laugh. Chaz and I laughed too and it didn't feel like my guts were about to fall out, which was nice. 'You guys!' the owner said and turned back to the bar, shaking his head.

'So, you going to go for it, or shall I?' I said to Chaz and nodded over to the two women. The more I looked at them, the more gorgeous they became.

'Why not both of us? Teamwork.'

'Fine,' I said. 'If you think you're up to it.'

Chaz snorted.

I led the way across the soft floor matting, the sand squeaking underfoot. We reached the bar and the women turned. I was just about to speak when a rush curtain three metres away was moved aside and two young guys, both smartly dressed up for the evening, ducked under and came in. The girls turned in unison. 'At last,' one of them declared. 'We were just about ready to give up on you two.'

Chaz and I had already turned one-eighty to head back towards our table. 'Oh, well!' I said with a shrug. 'You can't win them all.'

At the grand opening of a new luxury hotel in London, one uninvited guest plans to make this a day no one will ever forget

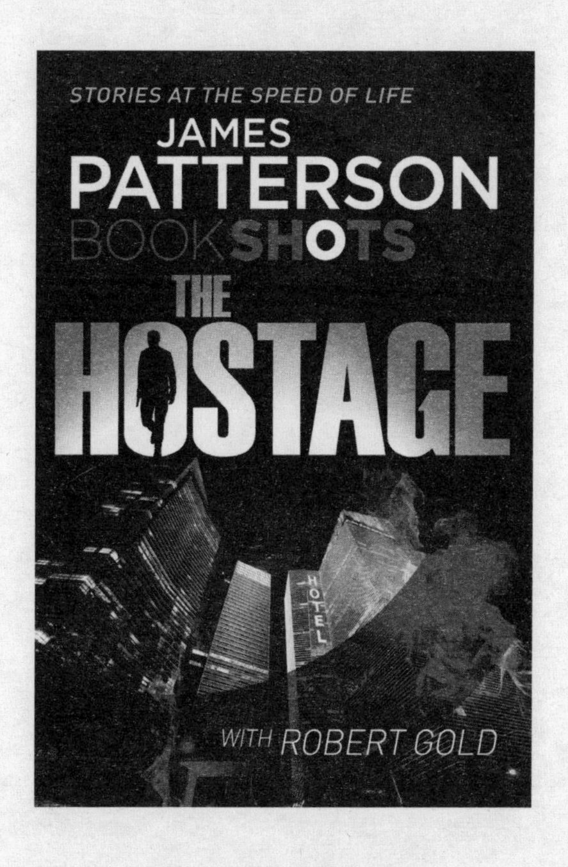

STORIES AT THE SPEED OF LIFE
JAMES
PATTERSON
BOOKSHOTS
THE
HOSTAGE
HOTEL
WITH ROBERT GOLD

Read on for an extract

Mayfair, London, 2016

Welcome, friends and honoured guests, to the brand-new Tribeca Luxury Hotel, here in the heart of the world-famous Mayfair district of London. Thirty years ago, in conjunction with my esteemed business partner, Oscar Miller, I opened the very first Tribeca Luxury Hotel in New York City. My aim today remains exactly as it was those thirty years ago – to deliver the ultimate in indulgence and service, set in the most opulent and tranquil surroundings.

When we opened our very first hotel, we placed our guests and the service we provided them at the very heart of everything we did. I am proud to say across our twenty-seven luxury hotels in operation around the world today, and of course in this, our twenty-eighth, that personal service remains. Every guest is treated as an individual and welcomed every time they visit as if they are returning to their very own home – the most luxurious home in the world.

In three days' time I will fulfil a lifelong ambition of opening a luxury hotel in Mayfair. For the very first time, we are bringing our unparalleled levels of exclusive accommodation, opulence and pure indulgence to the people of London and its international visitors. We take delight in offering our guests incomparable levels of comfort, consideration and security and our brand-new forty floors of palatial rooms are our finest demonstration of this yet.

I am honoured you are able to join us today at the exclusive preview of what I believe is the finest hotel in the world. Each one of you is my personal guest and I could not be more thrilled to welcome you to the new home of luxury in London, the Tribeca Hotel.

Jackson Harlington

Chairman, Tribeca Luxury Hotels

Stanley Samson stood in the marbled lobby and watched as each VIP guest was handed a branded magazine with a welcome letter from Jackson Harlington. This wasn't an event for ordinary travel writers. This wasn't even an event for the bosses of travel writers. This was an event for their bosses'

bosses. When it came to the grand opening of a Tribeca Luxury Hotel, Stanley knew that everyone wanted to attend and no one wanted to be overlooked.

Browsing through the magazine, guests would find a feature on each of the group's luxury hotels located around the world, from New York to Paris, Singapore to Beijing. But it went without saying the greatest prominence was given to this brand-new London hotel. Gatefold photographs captured the beauty of the interior and the amazing accommodation available to the richest and most famous in the world.

Stanley was aware years of preparation had gone into this day. Every exclusive suite individually styled, every room its own unique furniture, selected and purchased by the world's most renowned interior designers. Flowers adorned the hotel, with fresh bouquets in every room. Private chefs had been appointed to every suite and individual butlers would serve every treasured guest. On the fortieth floor an oasis of calm had been created with an infinity pool offering commanding views across London and into the neighbouring royal palace gardens. No expense had been spared in preparation for the opening of the new hotel. Everyone in London was talking about it and nobody wanted to miss out.

Before it even opened its doors, the hotel was fully booked for the next two years. Fully booked – unless you were the President of the United States, a member of the royal family or a superstar of international fame. For them, Tribeca Luxury Hotels prided itself on always having a suite available.

As the assistant to the Global Head of Security for the luxury hotel group, Stanley was waiting by the express glass elevator to accompany Jackson Harlington, his family and his business partner, Oscar Miller, across the marbled lobby of the hotel to its majestic new front entrance. There, Harlington and Miller would throw open the doors and invite inside the world's press, as they had at the grand opening of every single Tribeca Luxury Hotel for the past thirty years.

Stanley never failed to be amazed by each Tribeca hotel he visited around the world. Every one of them offered a higher level of luxury than the last. For Stanley, the hotels were beyond his wildest dreams and he appreciated every night he got to stay in one of the rooms – even if it was in a room reserved for staff guests.

Being present at the opening of a hotel in his home town made him feel particularly proud. He knew the London hotel was certain to be an enormous success and was delighted to be playing his small part in it. He looked out across the lobby, through its vast glass frontage, at the gathering crowd standing on the front lawns. Hearing the string quartet play, he watched as guests reached for their glasses of vintage champagne and foie gras canapés. For a moment he felt a slight pang of jealousy but contented himself with the thought of the freshly baked chocolate muffins being delivered to the kitchen later in the morning.

But as he closely watched events on the front lawn, Stanley had failed to notice that the express elevator had journeyed from the twenty-fifth to the thirty-eighth floor.

With a ski mask pulled tightly down across his face, an uninvited guest was dragging his petrified hostage down the hall on the thirty-eighth floor towards the Presidential Suite. The hostage had been pistol-whipped by his captor and was drifting in and out of consciousness. As the captor clicked open the door to the lavish suite, his hostage began to stir and became aware of his surroundings.

The captor didn't care.

His hostage's arms were tied at his wrists and his legs bound at his ankles. He threw the man face down onto the suite's super king bed, made up with the world's finest Egyptian cotton sheets. The hostage struggled to try to turn himself over. But as he rolled himself breathlessly onto his side, he was greeted by the sight of his captor standing over him. Picking up a heavy-duty rope from beside the bed, he was tying a hangman's noose.

Panic flooded across his body. Trapped and tied, he was physically defenceless. He knew his only hope was to talk to his captor.

'Tell me what you want. If it's money I will get whatever you ask for. I'm a wealthy man. I can get you anything. Absolutely anything. Just tell me what it is you want.'

In silence the captor continued to tie the noose.

The hostage sat himself upright on the bed.

'I can get you cash here today. Or I can put you on a plane to anywhere. Anywhere in the world. You hear me? I've more money than you could ever dream of!'

The captor tightened the noose.

'I said, did you hear me?' screamed the hostage. 'I have more money than you could ever dream of.'

The captor walked to the bed and struck his hostage on the side of the head, throwing him back down.

The noose was tied.

'Tell me what you want! You must want something? Make demands. Make them now. I can pay you. I'll pay you anything!'

But the captor had slipped the noose over his head and was dragging him to his feet. The hostage cried for help but it was hopeless. With the exception of the invited guests gathering thirty-eight floors below, the hotel was empty.

Being pulled like a dog, with the noose choking his airway, the hostage followed his captor out onto the balcony of the Presidential Suite.

*

Thirty-eight floors below, standing on the carefully manicured lawns, the gathering luminaries were being served the finest caviar, flown in from Russia that morning. Savouring every mouthful, their enjoyment was suddenly interrupted by an ear-splitting crash. Looking skywards, they saw shards of glass falling like ice towards the ground.

Standing on the edge of the balcony was a masked man with a hostage tied in a noose. Slowly, the man raised his knife and ripped through the shirt of his captive. In the gardens below, guests began to scream.

Forcing his hostage to his knees, his arms above his head, the captor tied his wrists tightly to the iron frame – all that remained of the Presidential balcony.

He secured the noose.

Then, with one kick, he pushed his hostage off the edge of the balcony, leaving the man hanging thirty-eight floors above the ground.

ON THE HOTEL LAWNS BELOW, cameras and smartphones turned upwards as the man swung from side to side. Stripped to his waist, his overfed figure exposed to the watching audience, he had no defence. Any attempt to escape now seemed futile, as he screamed in desperation at the crowd below.

Not wanting to keep his audience waiting, the masked man stepped forward and knelt closely beside his suspended hostage.

He was ready to continue the performance.

He raised his knife, its sharp blade glittering in the spring sun. The crowd gasped as, slowly, he pressed the knife against the man's face, letting it delicately cut his cheek as he edged it down towards his throat.

'Don't do this, don't do this,' gasped the hostage. 'It isn't too late. However much money you want I'll get it for you. Anything, absolutely anything. You can have it all. Do you hear me? Anything.'

The captor let the cold knife press deeper into his hostage's cheek before pushing his hidden mouth into his ear.

In a barely audible whisper, filled with hate, he spoke.

'That's a greedy gut, isn't it?'

He twisted the knife, dropping it down, cutting into the tight skin covering his hostage's obese stomach.

The hostage shrieked in pain as his captor rose up on his knees, reached skywards and showed the bloodied knife to the screaming crowd below.

It was time for the final act.

The captor pressed the knife against the rope that tied his hostage's wrists to the balcony frame. One cut of that rope and the man would be left hanging by the noose, thirty-eight floors above the ground.

The crowd gasped in fear and anticipation as the captor pressed harder and harder against the rope.

Then suddenly, sweeping the knife down to the hostage's stomach, he raced it back up through his torso, across his body, and spilt his entrails down towards the watching crowd below.

JAMES PATTERSON BOOKSHOTS

OUT THIS MONTH

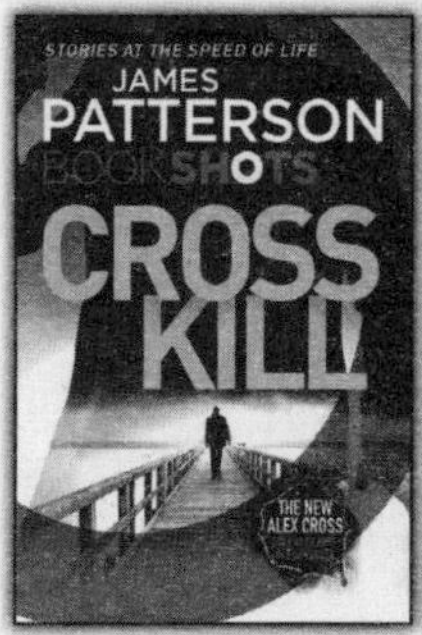

Along Came a Spider killer Gary Soneji died years ago. But Alex Cross swears he sees Soneji gun down his partner. Is his greatest enemy back from the grave?

Humans are evolving into a savage new species that could save civilisation – or end it. *Zoo* was just the beginning.

Detective Harry Blue is determined to take down the serial killer who's abducted several women, but her mission leads to a shocking revelation.

A royal is kidnapped the day before the Trooping the Colour parade. Can Private's Jack Morgan save the day before kidnap turns to murder?

A world-famous tennis player is stalked from Roland Garros to Wimbledon by a deadly killer intent on destroying more than just her career.

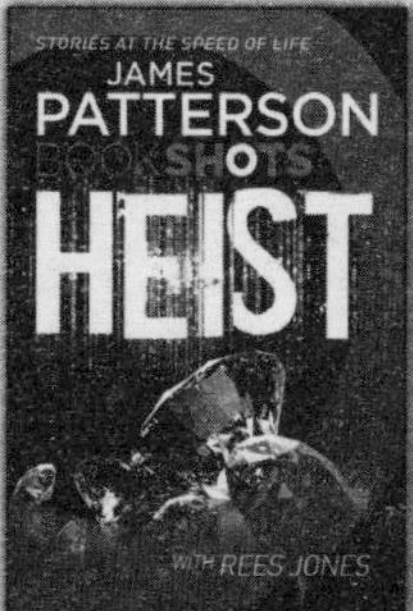

Two rival crews attempt to steal millions of pounds' worth of diamonds at exactly the same time, leading to a thrilling high-speed chase across Europe.

When former SAS captain David Shelley goes looking for a missing friend, he enters into the same danger that may have got his friend killed.

A man is thrown from the top floor of a glamorous new London hotel. Can Head of Security John Roscoe find the killer before the bodies pile up?

ALSO BY JAMES PATTERSON

ALEX CROSS NOVELS

Along Came a Spider
Kiss the Girls
Jack and Jill
Cat and Mouse
Pop Goes the Weasel
Roses are Red
Violets are Blue
Four Blind Mice
The Big Bad Wolf
London Bridges
Mary, Mary
Cross
Double Cross
Cross Country
Alex Cross's Trial (*with Richard DiLallo*)
I, Alex Cross
Cross Fire
Kill Alex Cross
Merry Christmas, Alex Cross
Alex Cross, Run
Cross My Heart
Hope to Die
Cross Justice

THE WOMEN'S MURDER CLUB SERIES

1st to Die
2nd Chance (*with Andrew Gross*)
3rd Degree (*with Andrew Gross*)
4th of July (*with Maxine Paetro*)
The 5th Horseman (*with Maxine Paetro*)
The 6th Target (*with Maxine Paetro*)
7th Heaven (*with Maxine Paetro*)
8th Confession (*with Maxine Paetro*)
9th Judgement (*with Maxine Paetro*)
10th Anniversary (*with Maxine Paetro*)
11th Hour (*with Maxine Paetro*)
12th of Never (*with Maxine Paetro*)
Unlucky 13 (*with Maxine Paetro*)
14th Deadly Sin (*with Maxine Paetro*)
15th Affair (*with Maxine Paetro*)

DETECTIVE MICHAEL BENNETT SERIES

Step on a Crack (*with Michael Ledwidge*)
Run for Your Life (*with Michael Ledwidge*)
Worst Case (*with Michael Ledwidge*)
Tick Tock (*with Michael Ledwidge*)
I, Michael Bennett (*with Michael Ledwidge*)
Gone (*with Michael Ledwidge*)
Burn (*with Michael Ledwidge*)
Alert (*with Michael Ledwidge*)

PRIVATE NOVELS

Private (*with Maxine Paetro*)
Private London (*with Mark Pearson*)

Private Games (*with Mark Sullivan*)
Private: No. 1 Suspect (*with Maxine Paetro*)
Private Berlin (*with Mark Sullivan*)
Private Down Under (*with Michael White*)
Private L.A. (*with Mark Sullivan*)
Private India (*with Ashwin Sanghi*)
Private Vegas (*with Maxine Paetro*)
Private Sydney (*with Kathryn Fox*)
Private Paris (*with Mark Sullivan*)

NYPD RED SERIES

NYPD Red (*with Marshall Karp*)
NYPD Red 2 (*with Marshall Karp*)
NYPD Red 3 (*with Marshall Karp*)
NYPD Red 4 (*with Marshall Karp*)

STAND-ALONE THRILLERS

Sail (*with Howard Roughan*)
Swimsuit (*with Maxine Paetro*)
Don't Blink (*with Howard Roughan*)
Postcard Killers (*with Liza Marklund*)
Toys (*with Neil McMahon*)
Now You See Her (*with Michael Ledwidge*)
Kill Me If You Can (*with Marshall Karp*)
Guilty Wives (*with David Ellis*)
Zoo (*with Michael Ledwidge*)
Second Honeymoon (*with Howard Roughan*)
Mistress (*with David Ellis*)
Invisible (*with David Ellis*)
The Thomas Berryman Number
Truth or Die (*with Howard Roughan*)
Murder House (*with David Ellis*)

NON-FICTION

Torn Apart (*with Hal and Cory Friedman*)
The Murder of King Tut (*with Martin Dugard*)

ROMANCE

Sundays at Tiffany's (*with Gabrielle Charbonnet*)
The Christmas Wedding (*with Richard DiLallo*)
First Love (*with Emily Raymond*)

OTHER TITLES

Miracle at Augusta (*with Peter de Jonge*)